A LEADER IN TH

A LEADER IN THE CHALET SCHOOL

Elinor M. Brent-Dyer

Armada

First published in the U.K. in 1961 by
W. & R. Chambers Ltd., Edinburgh.
First published in Armada in 1985 by
Fontana Paperbacks,
8 Grafton Street, London W1X 3LA.

© Elinor M. Brent-Dyer 1961

Printed in Great Britain by
William Collins Sons & Co. Ltd., Glasgow.

Dedicated to my friend and editor
Mr John L. Blair, with thanks for much
patience and many kindnesses

CONTENTS

Chapter 1

JACK

JACK stood in the middle of her cubicle and looked round, taking it all in. Her eyes danced delightedly and her lips stretched almost literally from ear to ear in one broad grin. This was the Chalet School and she was here at last!

Her elder sister, Anne, was there too, but Anne didn't really count over this in Jack's estimation. When their parents had issued a fiat that the Chalet School must wait until Jack was eleven, Anne had accepted it in her usual quiet way. But Jack had made a complete nuisance of herself until one night when Dad, having put up with all the teasing he meant to, pulled her up short and sharp.

"OK—OK!" he said when nine-year-old Jack had been pestering as usual. "You want to go to the Chalet School. Now listen to me, young woman! Go on like this, never giving anyone any peace on the subject, and, so far as you are concerned, it'll be never! Got that?"

Jack was silenced, though she didn't really believe it. Later on, however, when she was in bed, Mother came up for the usual ten minutes' talk before she put out the light, and she told her small daughter very firmly that Dad meant every word.

"But he couldn't!" Jack had gasped. "You've always promised that Anne and I should go to the Chalet School and I'm dying for it after all Auntie Gay and Auntie Jacynth have told us about it. You can't go back on a promise!"

"We're not." Mother replied. "We promised that you should go when you were eleven and that's not for two years yet. If you're going to go on making such a complete

7

pest of yourself, this is one time when we both can and will break it. If you go on tormenting about it, when the time comes, Anne shall go and you will stay at home and go to the High School."

No one heard a single remark from her, nor did her parents mention the Chalet School again until her eleventh birthday, which happened on August Ist.

She had her reward at bedtime when Mother, coming to say good night and ask if it had been a happy birthday, crowned everything by telling her that all was arranged. She and Anne were going to Switzerland when the Christmas term began in September.

And then, exactly a week before term began, their brother Bobby went down with mumps! Jack followed suit three weeks later and Anne started on the very day before quarantine was up. By the time all infection was at an end, it was half term and Dad said they must wait for the Easter term. Anne had been really ill for some days. The doctor advised a change of air before she went back to school, and Mother had taken them to Torquay to stay with Uncle Paul and Auntie Jan who had no children of their own and made a corresponding fuss over their nieces and nephews.

There had been one very good thing about it. In the beginning, Mother had left buying their uniforms till the last week because both were growing up so quickly. Mumps had intensified the growing and if those uniforms had been bought earlier, they would have had to be let down and taken in, for Anne, who had been plump before her illness, was positively scraggy and even Jack had lost weight. Now, they could get the uniform to fit properly. What was more, during the Christmas term, the Chalet School had decided to give up gym tunics and have a proper frock instead. It mattered much more to Anne who, at fourteen, was growing clothes-conscious. Jack's preferred attire was jeans and a jumper.

She had reached this point in her thoughts when the pretty, pansy-sprinkled curtains of her cubicle were parted and the big girl who had explained that she was dormitory

8

prefect for Pansy this term, and who had taken charge of the excited Jack, looked in.

"Ready?" she asked. "Then come along with me and I'll hand you over to—let me see—Wanda von Eschenau, I think. You're eleven, aren't you?"

Jack nodded violently. The big girl, who had introduced herself as Len Maynard, grinned. "That means Lower IIIa, I expect, which is Wanda's form. Likewise, she's in this dormy—next door to you. She's been at the school more than a year now and knows all the ropes. She's a jolly decent kid and I think you'll like her. Come on with me and meet her and see what you think about it. Oh, and while I remember, once you're down, you're down till bedtime, so make sure you've got all you want. Clean hanky and so on."

Jack produced a spotless handkerchief and Len nodded. "Good! This way! We always use the back stairs. Only school prefects and staff use the front. Wanda will be in the Junior Middles' common room by this time and so will all the rest. You people came late."

"Dad had to go to Basle on business for his firm," Jack explained as she followed Len down the corridor, "so he brought us as far as that with him in the car. What a queer name that Wanda person has! And I say! What a gorgeous floor for sliding!"

Len looked down at her with a laugh. "I don't advise you to try it on. Matey would have heaps to say and none of it nice! You leave the corridors alone!"

Jack heard her with perhaps half an ear. Her mind had gone back to the girl who was to "show her the ropes."

"Is the Wanda girl a foreigner?" she queried as she skipped down the stairs after Len. "My Auntie Gay told me that there would be heaps of foreigners at the school, now it's moved back to the Alps. She said there were scarcely any when she went to it. That was in England, of course."

"Gay?" Len stopped dead. "And your name's Lambert, isn't it? Do you mean to tell me that Gay Lambert is your

9

aunt? The one who was at the school when it was at Plas Howell in Armishire? Are you her niece?"

"Of course I am," Jack replied readily. "She isn't Gay Lambert any more, or course. She's married and has twins—Ruth, after Mother, and Jill, whose real name is Gillian, after another pal of hers—a Miss Culver. I used to wish I was twins," she went on conversationally, "Anne and Bobby are years older than me, you see."

"Not so much if your Anne is the new girl in Upper IVb. They're mostly around fourteen there."

"Fourteen's a lot older when the other one of you is eleven," Jack argued, "and Bobby is nearly sixteen!"

"I suppose it could be—though we haven't found it so. But tell me, Jack, when was Gay married? This, my child, is NEWS!"

"Two years ago. Anne and I were her bridesmaids."

"But why on earth didn't she let us know at school? The last we heard of her was that she was teaching in Australia. Is she still there?"

"Oh, yes. They live in Melbourne—at least, it's ten miles or so outside. Did you know Auntie Gay when she was at school, then?"

"I did. I was only a K.G. baby and Gay was a prefect; but I knew her all right. But we can't stop here nattering just now. I must hear all the latest some time when there's a moment to spare. You come on and meet your form."

Len laid a hand on Jack's shoulder and steered her round a corner. "This way! It's muddling, at first, with all the corridors built on to link up places, but you'll soon be able to find your way about. Oh, and while I think of it, I know rules are in abeyance today—I mean," as she caught Jack's puzzled look, "that they aren't in full swing until tomorrow, and the languages one not until Monday. All the same, it's as well to begin early. One important rule is no talking on the stairs or in the corridors."

"But you get that at any school," Jack said wisely. "Miss Ward at Redfearn House explained to us that you had to have it or the noise would be terrific."

10

"How right she was! This is the Junior Middles' common room. You'll be spending a lot of your free time here this term. In the summer, of course, we're outdoors most of the time. Come along and we'll see if we can grab Wanda."

Len opened the door on a buzz of conversation. She stood looking round for her quarry while Jack stared round, taking in all she could see.

The room was a large, pleasant one, with pale yellow walls. Prints of famous pictures hung round three of them. The fourth held the windows which at present were shrouded with curtains of a warm, glowing orange. Along two of the walls ran low bookcases, crowded and crammed with books of all kinds that folk who had not yet reached the teen age would like. Jack glanced at them carelessly. She was not much of a reader, being one of the active kind.

There were several chairs and two huge settees, one at each side of a tall, white-tiled object which intrigued Jack hugely. She was to find out later that it was a stove and was largely responsible for the pleasant warmth of the room. There were a couple of long tables, one fitted up for table tennis and the other clearly for other table games. In a corner stood half a dozen folding card-tables besides. A long door gave promise of a cupboard and Jack found later that it contained games, jigsaw puzzles and piles of the most delightful scrapbooks, which were a joy to everyone. The floor had a scatter of gay rugs over the polished boards and the room was well lit. Altogether, a most satisfying room for people of their age!

By this time, Len had found the girl she wanted, one of a huddle of ten all squashed together on one of the settees, and how they managed it only they themselves knew. Len called the one she wanted and then turned back to the door where Jack still stood.

"Here you are!" she said. "Wanda, this is the new girl, Jack Lambert. Jack, this is Wanda von Eschenau who will do sheepdog for you for the first few days until you've

11

found your feet. I don't know if you speak anything but your own language—"

"I don't," Jack said in a hurry, and rather appalled. "Have we got to?"

"But yes; but you will soon learn, for we will all help you," Wanda herself said in friendly tones. "Len, did you say her name is Jack? But always I have thought that in English that is a boy's name."

"It's Jacynth, really," Jack answered for herself, while she stared in amazement at Wanda. "I'm called after two of my aunts, Jacynth Gabrielle. Aunt Jacynth lives with us when she's at home— she plays the 'cello at concerts, and she's often away on tours—so Dad said I'd better be shortened, so they made it 'Jack'. That lady I saw in the office when we came said I could be Jack here, too. Please don't call me Jacynth. I loathe it!"

"But I like Jack," Wanda said. "It suits you. Oh, no; you could never be Jacynth. You are not at all like it—is she, Len?"

Len laughed as she surveyed Jack with her cropped black hair; her cheeky small face with dancing black eyes; her distinctly boyish stance, feet apart, hands in pockets.

"She's Jack all right," she said, "though I hadn't given it a thought till you spoke. All the same, Jack, I'd keep my hands out of my pockets, if I were you. If Matey catches you at that game, she'll sew your pockets up. Look after her, Wanda, and tell her what she wants to know. I expect she'll be in your form and she's in Pansy in the cubicle next to yours. I'll see you later, Jack. If Wanda can't answer your questions, you may ask me when we meet and I'll do my best for you. Goodbye now!"

Len slipped out, leaving Jack to find her own feet with the help of Wanda and the rest of Lower IIIa. As she went to join her own clan, she thought, "Wanda's right! The name doesn't suit her in the least! She's a Jack all over! Much more like a boy than a girl! What a contrast to Wanda!" with a fleeting memory of that small person's fairytale loveliness of golden curls, violet eyes and perfect

12

features and complexion. "She and Wanda ought to be rather good for each other. Well, now to go and announce the latest news about Gay!"

She had reached the Senior common room by this time and she opened the door and walked in, to be welcomed vociferously by her own crowd. She grinned at them, mounted a chair and announced loudly, "To all who knew Gay Lambert when she was at school at Plas Howell! Her two nieces are here. What's more, she's married now, and has twin girls of her own!"

The hubbub which followed this dramatic statement was momentous. Quite a number of the Seniors had been in the Chalet School Kindergarten when Gay Lambert had been a Senior herself.

Len contrived to forget quite comfortably all about Jack Lambert for the time being and, in any case, apart from dormitory contacts, she hardly thought it likely that she would have much to do with a Junior Middle. Therein, she was completely wrong, as she was to find out. Jack was to cling to her like a limpet and she was to stand up for Jack, tooth and nail, even when things looked very black for that insouciant young person.

Chapter 2

JACK TRIES WINTER SPORTS

BY the time Saturday morning arrived, Jack was settling down very comfortably— much more so than Anne, who was shy and reserved by nature and slow to make friends. Len had met her and was greatly intrigued to see that so far as looks were concerned, she was not in the least like Jack. Anne was blue-eyed, brown-haired and had the makings of a very attractive girl by the time she was grown up. But the difference was in far more than looks. Anne was quiet and retiring, apt to go with the crowd and little given to voicing her opinions aloud. Jack was keen, eager, a real live wire. She said exactly what she thought, whether it was likely to meet with approval from the rest or not. Some of them liked her on sight. One or two actively disliked her. But you could never ignore her. The staff found that out very quickly and so did the Junior Middles.

As Len had guessed, Jack was placed in Lower IIIa and soon proved that she was quite equal to the work if she chose. Anne, in Upper IVb, made far less impression on everyone, though she soon got the reputation for being a slogger. She and Jack saw comparatively little of each other. There were four forms between them, since Lower Fourth had two divisions as well. Apart from that, they were in different Houses, Jack being in Ste Thérèse de Lisieux and Anne in St. Clare's.

As for Len, if she thought that a member of Va was unlikely to have much to do with a Junior Middle out of dormitory, that was where she was mistaken, as she soon found out. Jack meant to come to her when she needed

14

information or advice and did so. In vain the rest of the form, shocked at her informality, told her that Wanda was "sheep-dogging" her and it was to Wanda she should go. Jack refused to listen.

"I know Wanda says she'll show me the ropes," she told Renata van Buren when that young woman had taken her aside to air her views on the subject. "She has, too. Wanda's a peach! She has my vote every time! But there are lots of things it wouldn't be much use asking her about, for she wouldn't know the answers—or if she did, they might be the wrong ones. Len's my own dormitory prefect, so I've every right to ask her and I shall."

"And that's exactly what she does do!" Len wailed to her sister Con one Sunday when they were walking to early Mass in the school's own chapel. "She can't get at me much during the day, but she saves up every blessed thing and asks me in the dorm. I wouldn't mind once or twice, but so far it's been every day. It's the outside of enough!"

Con gave her sister an odd look. As Len had told Jack, she was one of a set of triplets. The other two were Con and, left in San on this occasion, thanks to a handsome black eye sustained when she had heedlessly run into an open door, Margot. At one time, the three had been inseparable. Nowadays, they had branched off with friends of their own and were growing apart a little. But the two eldest of the triplets had always been very close and even now, with different friends, they remained much closer than either did with Margot, who was apt to be a lone wolf in some ways.

"I suppose it was bound to happen sooner or later," Con said, hugging herself closer in her heavy coat and scarf.

"Bound to happen! What on earth do you mean?" Len demanded.

"What I say. You've always been the leader of us three— of the whole family, if it comes to that. Even the boys—even young Mike—listen to you. I expect it was bound to come out at school, too. You've led the form quite a good deal, especially this last year or so."

Len nearly dropped her torch—it was not quite a quarter to eight and still very dark up on the Görnetz Platz—as she turned to her sister with a shiver induced by the cold of late January. "Do you mean that I'm getting *bossy*? For pity's sake, Con, if you see any signs of that happening, choke me off at once! I haven't forgotten all Mary-Lou had to say to me last summer term! I'm not giving anyone the chance to talk to me like that again! Once was enough! I never felt so awful in my life!"

"Pipe down, idiot! I didn't mean anything of the kind. All I meant was that you come to the front every time —can't help it. It's what Papa calls part of your make-up. Other people feel it and turn to you for help and advice—I do myself. If ever I'm stuck I always ask you. It's like Mamma, you know. The same thing happens to her. It seems to me," Con finished as they reached the door of the chapel, "that if you're like that, you've just got to lend a hand when it's asked. Hard luck on you and I'm glad it's not me. But there it is."

"But what am I to do? That kid asks me the most unearthly questions!" Len complained. "I don't mind about school things, but she doesn't stop there."

"You'll have to pray about it, I expect," Con said as she pushed the door open. "Anyhow, if young Jack has decided to take you for her Nanny, I expect you'll have to be it. She's obstinate and someone will have to keep her on the rails or goodness knows what will happen!"

They were inside now, so talking ceased, and when the service was over other folk joined them and no more was said on the subject. Once they were back in school, Len had to rush upstairs and make sure that her dormitory had performed all its duties. She had been head of Gentian the term before and Betty Landon had been in Pansy. But Betty had not been a success as dormitory prefect. She was far too heedless herself to be much help with a set of harum-scarum youngsters. So she and Len had been changed, much to Len's disgust.

Pansy was given over to Junior Middles, including Jack, Wanda, Renata van Buren, Arda Peik, another Dutch girl, a delicate child, Gretchen von Ahlen whose mother was one of Mrs. Maynard's closest friends, a French girl, Ghislaine Touvet, and another English girl, Rosemary Wentworth. To these eleven-year-olds Len, at fifteen, seemed almost grown-up and, for the most part, they regarded her with a certain wholesome awe.

Len, making the rounds, found that the term was still new enough for everyone to have fulfilled her duties properly. She hung away her hat and coat in the closet and proceeded to marshal her lambs downstairs.

Jack was at the tail of the line and as she passed the dormitory prefect, she broke away long enough to hiss in a half-whisper, "I want to speak to you, please. When can I?"

"Not till after Frühstück and all our chores are done," Len replied. "Get back into line, Jack, and hurry up. You're holding up the people from Crocus."

Jack slipped back into her place and Len, with a final look round, switched off the lights and followed them downstairs. She saw the party safely into their common room and then departed to join her own crowd. Con came up to her.

"I've been up to San," she said. "Margot's head has stopped aching, but her eye looks awful! It's just as well Mamma's away in Basle for the next week. She'd have a fit if she saw it! Nurse says that if we and Ruey like, we can go to San and have Kaffee und Kuchen with Margot this afternoon. I said we would. That's OK, isn't it?"

"Of course!" Len said. "Poor old Margot! She does get into the wars!" She turned to the girl who had followed Con and was grinning at her. "Hello, Rue! Heard the plan for this afternoon?"

Ruey nodded. "Con told me. Are you letting Auntie Jo know later?"

"We'll have to, if Matey doesn't. But I expect she will. Anyhow, it's nothing to worry about—just a black eye. We needn't rush to do it. Mother has her hands full with Geoff and Phil teething their heads off as well you know! If you're writing to her today, don't say anything about it."

"I'm not. I'm writing to Roger and Roddy and that'll do me. But if either of you are writing give her my love."

The sound of the gong put a stop to further conversation, and the Seniors lined up and marched off to the Speisesaal.

As it turned out, there was no time for Jack to consult Len on whatever point was exercising her mind just then. When the meal was nearly over, the bell on the staff table sounded sharply, stilling the noise of chatter and laughter. The girls all turned to look up the long room to where the Head was standing smiling at them and her first words brought corresponding smiles from everyone present.

"One moment, girls! We have been promised a fine day at last and the snow is in grand condition. When you come back from Church, all change into skiing suits as fast as you can and you may spend the rest of the morning outdoors. Have your skis and sticks and toboggans ready so that we can get off with no waste of time. Especially don't forget your snow-goggles. We don't want any cases of snow blindness if we can help it. Finally, remember that when the whistle blows, you are to stop whatever you are doing and line up instantly. Don't forget! Now that is all!"

She sat down to finish her coffee and roll while the chatter broke out again. Even the prefects were excited, for this was the first chance they had had this term for winter sports. They had had none the previous term, and since they had come back the weather had been so uncertain that they had only been allowed short walks along the road. No one was going to risk having a crowd of girls out in a snow flurry that might turn to a minor blizzard before you could look round!

18

Jack was so thrilled by the prospect that she forgot what it was she wanted to ask Len about, and gabbled excitedly to Wanda, Arda and Renata as she finished her meal.

"Can we choose whether we ski or toboggan?" she demanded

"Of course," Wanda told her. "Which will you choose, Jack?"

Jack considered. "I don't really know. I'd love to have a shot at skiing 'cos I've never done it before. But it might be easier just to coast. Only, what do we do for sledges? We haven't any."

"Some of us have and there are the school toboggans," Renata said between two bites of a roll that was literally oozing honey. "I'll ski, I think. It's such gorgeous fun, once you've got your balance and I'm dying to see if I've still got mine. It only came at the end of the snow last year. You've got skis, haven't you, Jack? Then do that and we'll give you a hand at the beginning."

"I wish I could go like Mlle," Arda remarked wistfully. "It looks lovely when she does it. She just skims over the ground! So do a lot of the prees and the big girls. You wait till you see Josette Russell!"

"That's the Head Girl, isn't it?" Jask asked as she set down her empty cup.

"Yes; and she's simply marvellous at skiing! Of course, she's been here for years and she often stays for a week or two with the Maynards in the Christmas hols. They're cousins, you know."

"Renata! That honey's going to drop on your frock in a minute!" Rosemary Wentworth exclaimed.

Renata settled that by cramming the last half bodily into her mouth, thus gagging herself most effectually. Jack, meanwhile, had given Arda a startled look.

"Do you mean Josette is a cousin of the Maynards?" she asked in awed tones.

Arda nodded "And Ailie Russell from Upper IVb. Oh, and Maeve Bettany in VIb is another. Lady Russell

19

who started the school is their aunt. She was Miss Bettany then and so was Mrs Maynard."

"Crumbs! I never knew that!" was all Jack could find to say. Then she added, "But I thought the boss of the school was the person you all call 'Madame'? Who's she?"

"That is Lady Russell," Renata explained, having finally swallowed her mouthful. Then she choked on a crumb which had gone down the wrong way.

By the time her neighbours had thumped her back with hearty goodwill and the prefect in charge, Barbara Chester, had come to see what was wrong, Renata was red and her eyes were streaming. Barbara fetched her more coffee and made her sip it slowly. Before she had recovered, most of the other tables had been cleared and Lower IIIa alone were left. They had to hurry, for Karen, the ruler of the kitchen regions, was apt to be cross if she was held up. Then they had a scramble to get ready for church, so even if Jack could have caught Len, there would have been no time for talk. As it happened, that young person had been called to the study to take a telephone call from her mother in Basle and Pansy never saw their prefect until they were all setting off for church.

The Protestant service ended five minutes before the Catholic one did. It was a bitterly cold day and the staff allowed no loitering. They hustled their girls off with orders to change quickly and be ready to set off as fast as possible. The weather prophets might foretell a fine day, but the sun they had promised had not appeared so far and, as Miss Annersley had reminded her staff, you can never rely on anything in the Alps when it comes to weather!

The unwritten law of the school was that during the Christmas and Easter terms the girl were to be outdoors whenever possible. A good many of them had relatives in the great Sanatorium at the other end of the Görnetz Platz and health came first every time at the Chalet School.

Jack finally opted for skis and she appeared in the narrow walk between the school and the shrubbery, clad in her smart blue skisuit with its cosy hood protecting her ears from frostbite, her big boots, properly nailed, and crimson mitts. Her snow goggles were perched on her small nose and she carried skis in one hand and sticks in the other. She was almost the last to appear.

"Now are you all ready?" demanded Miss Carey, their form mistress. "Then come along and hurry up! Nearly everyone else has gone already."

Thanking her stars that Sundays were go-as-you-please so far as languages was concerned, Jack turned to Wanda, who was partnering her, to ask eagerly for tips about skiing.

"But when we arrive at our ground we will show you," Wanda returned. "That will be easier than telling you. But one thing I must say, and that is you must remember to keep the points of your skis from crossing."

"How?" Jack demanded, staring.

"You will see," was all she got; and in any case, Miss Carey was hurrying them at such a rate that no one had much breath for talking. Walking over the frozen snow, even in properly nailed boots, was an effort. Jack gave all her mind to it, and by the time they had arrived her cheeks were crimson and she would dearly have liked to throw back her hood. The first hint, however, brought a shower of horrified exclamations, and she was given to understand that if she did, she would be sent back to school for Matron to deal with.

"But why?" she demanded. "What harm could it do? I couldn't take cold! I'm just about boiling!"

"Mais, tes oreilles!" exclaimed Ghislaine Touvet. "Elles iront à geler!"

Jack, whose French was not equal to this, turned to Wanda. "What's she say?"

"She says," Wanda returned with a giggle, "that your ears will freeze. Truly, Jack, you must not. Strap on the skis instead and Renata and I will show you what to do. Come on! Make haste!"

Jack did as she was told and presently stood up, the skis

21

strapped to her feet, a stick in either hand, and looked at her teachers, who closed in one on each side of her.

"Do not lift your feet," Wanda instructed her. "Slide them forward—first one and then the other. And try to slide them straight."

Thus urged, Jack cautiously obeyed. She did it three times and then the inevitable happened. As if magnetised, the points slid together and over she went with a wild yell.

She was not hurt and the other two got her to her feet at once.

"Try again!" Arda said. "It's the only way, Jack. Truly it is."

Jack tried again—and again—and yet again. It all seemed no use. Do as she would, those wretched points rushed together sooner or later.

"I don't believe I'll ever do it!" she said desperately at last.

"But yes; you will," Wanda said instantly. "It is what happens to us all—even Mlle!"

Jack glanced across the meadow to where Mlle, looking like a small scarlet bird, was racing with two of the prefects, and heaved such a deep sigh that she nearly blew the fairylike Wanda away. "I just can't believe it! She must have been born on skis!"

"Now then, you two, Wanda and Renata," said a well-known voice behind them, "how much skiing for yourselves have you had? None? Then be off and have a good run to warm up and I'll see to Jack!"

The three turned—with fatal effect on Jack. Down she went, but this time it was Len who hauled her up and set her on her feet before she waved the other two off firmly. "Be off with you both! Wanda, you're looking cold. See that she gets well warmed up, Renata! Now, Jack!" as Wanda and Renata finally sped off, side by side.

"I'll never do it!" Jack wailed.

"Oh, yes; you will," said someone else who had come

up at this moment. "Look at me! I'd never been on skis in my life till this winter and I can get along after a fashion now. Shall I give you a hand with her, Len?"

"No; I think I can manage better alone," Len said. "Besides, though you can manage, Ruey, you're not sure yet. You go off and practise and I'll take Jack for a few minutes' intensive coaching!"

Ruey laughed, said encouragingly "Stick to it, Jack!", swerved round them and was off after Con who was practising turns by herself.

Len could teach: not a doubt of it! Wanda and Renata had told Jack to slide but they had forgotten to tell her to bend her knees with each movement. Len explained and it certainly helped a little. Then Jack was warned against trying to keep her body upright unless she was finishing a turn and presently, she found that thanks to all this she had managed seven steps forward before she fell once more.

"But I managed seven!" she said triumphantly as Len helped her up.

Len laughed. "Oh, you're making progress. Now try by yourself for a few minutes while I go and see what those kids are doing."

She left Jack to it while she skimmed over to a small crowd of Second Formers who seemed to be tying themselves into knots over something. Jack set off again, and had only gone down twice when the Head Girl herself appeared and proceeded to take her briskly in hand.

"One of us would have taken you over sooner," she explained, "but we saw that first two of your own crowd and then Len were seeing to you."

"Yes, thank you," Jack said, very shyly for her. She had fully imbibed the feeling rampant among the small fry that the Head Girl was someone really out of sight and the prefects not much nearer. And then she got a shock, for Con Maynard came flying along to say "I'll take over now if you like, Josette, and you scram and see what those ghastly Inter V folk are after. If they go on yelling like that, our fun will be cut short. Just listen!"

There was some reason for her remarks. The yells proceeding from the far side of the meadow might have been heard almost down to the valley!

"Oh, drat them! It's Prudence and Co., of course!" Josette exclaimed as she spun round and went flying over the snow. Con looked after her with a chuckle.

"Poor old Josette! It's a hard life and she always did like to take things gently. Come on, Jack! Get a move on! I'll give you a hand."

Between them all, by the time the whistle blew the recall, Jack was beginning to find her balance in real earnest. She was good at all games and once she had fully grasped what was needed, she managed much better, though she was very unsteady still.

"But I'll do it if I bust!" she assured Wanda and Renata later when they were all in the common room, waiting for the gong to sound for Mittagessen, as she had learned to call the midday meal. "I say, Wanda! Do you know, Con talked to the Head Girl as if she was just anyone!"

"What of it?" demanded Margaret Twiss, another member of IIIa who happened to overhear. "They're cousins—don't you know that yet?"

"Wanda told me this morning. But the Head Girl!"

"She's just another girl," Margaret said shortly. Josette had pulled her up for untidiness the morning before and had pointed out sharply that it was early in the term for this sort of thing. "She's just a little older than we are and she's in VIa, but that's all. Anyhow," she added. "I never have thought it was fair that *she* was made Head Girl. I think Gwen Parry or Clare Kennedy would have been heaps better. Only of course she's Madame's daughter, so I s'pose they felt they had to do it."

While Jack stared, Renata replied to this smartly. "That had nothing to do with it or Sybil would have been Head Girl when she was in the Sixth and she never was. You've a good cheek to talk like that, Margaret Twiss!" (It was a source of wonder to a good many folk that Renata not only spoke English fluently, but was equally fluent in English slang!)

Margaret flushed, and it was just as well that the gong sounded at that moment, for quite half of them were ruffling their feathers like so many little turkey cocks and there was every prospect of trouble. But the gong put an end to it and as Miss Carey elected to take the head of their table for once, there was no chance of recurring to it during the meal. So it passed over for the time being.

Chapter 3

NIGHT-TIME ADVENTURE

AFTER all Jack had no chance that day to tackle Len about the questions that were worrying her. After Mittagessen, the two Maynards and Ruey Richardson disappeared from public view. Jack, very disgruntled, had to make the best of it, and when Rosemary asked why she was in such a gloom, she got the very dignified reply, "I'm thinking."

"Don't hurt yourself!" jeered Margaret who overheard this. "D'you always look so down in the mouth when you're thinking? Snap out of it, Jack!"

Jack made no reply, but she got up from her seat near the stove and marched over to the window, whither no one was likely to follow her on such a cold day, and remained there. Only the arrival of Miss Bertram who was on duty and who had come to read to them shifted her. Miss Bertram was not allowing any girl to remain out of the circle and called Jack to join the others and be quick.

Her gloom returned full force when she learned that Len had gone with the others to Benediction which meant that she would be back only in time for Abendessen. Immediately after that came school Prayers and then bed for everyone of twelve or under. By the time the Seniors came upstairs everyone in Pansy was asleep, cuddled down under the blankets and plumeaux.

Len peeped into Jack's cubicle, for she had not forgotten the younger girl's request, but Jack was sleeping as soundly as the rest and Len knew better than to wake her.

"She'll just have to wait till tomorrow," Len thought with a slight shiver. "Anyhow, I'm not anxious to have some of her wild questions shot at me at this time of night. Brr! How cold it is! Bed for mine, and in short order!"

There was central heating in all the dormitories, but the bitter chill of the night seemed to be beating even that. Len knelt down and said her prayers first and then undressed and snuggled down in bed as fast as she could go.

She fell asleep almost at once, but halfway through the night, she roused. How ghastly cold it was! Even with all the warm blankets and feather plumeau usually guaranteed to keep out the cold of an Alpine winter night, she was shivery. She got up and found her dressing gown and rolled herself tightly in that.

"Wish I had a hot bottle!" she thought. "I could do with it for once!"

Then she heard movements from one of the other cubicles and instantly sat up and felt for the torch she kept under her pillow in case of need. She shuffled her feet into her bedroom slippers and, as an afterthought, hauled the top blanket off the bed and wrapped that round her. Then she padded forth to see what was wrong.

All was as usual until she reached Jack's cubicle. There, she found that young woman trying to get into her underclothes as well as she could in the dark. She jumped when Len and her torch appeared.

"Oh, I'm so glad to see someone!" she exclaimed as well as she could for chattering teeth.

"Sh! Don't wake the others!" Len said imperatively. "What's the matter with you, Jack? Are you ill?"

"I'm so c-co-old!" Jack shivered. "Is it often as c-c-cold as this?"

"Not often," Len replied. "Put on your dressing gown and get back into bed and I'll tuck you up."

Jack obeyed her meekly and Len tucked her junior in firmly. "Now stay where you are," she said, speaking in the undertone which never carried as a whisper would. "I'm going to see Matey for a moment, so don't try to get out again. She may come back with me."

That was quite hint enough for Jack who had once—and only once!—tried to argue with Matron. She snuggled down comfortably and waited.

Len left the cubicle and made for the big radiator against the opposite wall. As a rule at this hour it was comfortably warm. Tonight it was stone cold. Something was wrong with the central heating and she must report it at once. Quite apart from the crops of colds and chills that might follow if she left it, the radiators would freeze and a nice thing that would be!

She slipped out of the dormitory into the silent corridor. Down the stairs she tiptoed and along to Matron's room. She tapped lightly on the door, but no reply came. Greatly daring, she opened the door a crack and listened. Something in the silence told her that Matron was not there, so she went in, switching on the light.

"Now what do I do?" Len demanded of the empty room. "Matey may have found out about the heating; or she may just have been yanked out to someone being sick or having a pain."

After consideration, she decided that just in case Matron had been called to some sufferer and knew nothing about the heating, she had better go hunting. The room was warm, so evidently it was only part of the building that was affected.

"Best go down and see if Matey is on to it already," Len finally decided. She pulled up her blanket round her, quitted the room, and set off on her journey to the kitchens. The boiler room led off from the far end of the kitchen premises, so if it was the heating Matron was after that was where she was most likely to be.

The kitchens were very cosy, for the big slow-combustion stoves were never let out during termtime. Len switched on the lights and went through to the boiler room. Matron was not there; nor, to judge by what she could feel and hear, was there anything wrong with the furnaces. She was afraid to open the doors in case she let loose a cascade of hot ash, so she finally retraced her path.

28

"Someone must be sick," she thought as she reached the foot of the stairs. "Oh, glory! That means chasing round the dormies till I find her! What a job!"

She was beginning to turn drowsy, which might have been the reason why, halfway up the long flight of stairs, she tripped on a corner of her blanket and slipped. She grabbed at the handrail and saved herself, but in doing so dropped her torch. It went clattering down the uncarpeted stairs, making a noise that, to its startled owner, was enough to waken the dead, let alone the school!

Len clung to the rail and held her breath, waiting for an outcry. It didn't come, but the noise attracted the very person she was hunting. Matron, clad in dressing gown and slippers, appeared in a flash at the head of the stairs, her own torch in her hand. She shone it down the stairs, demanding imperatively, "Who is there? Come up here at once, whoever you are!"

"It's only me, Matron," Len said meekly, yanking up her blanket and going upstairs as fast as she could.

"Len Maynard! What on earth are you doing downstairs at this hour?" Matron exclaimed. Then her expression changed. "Con isn't sleepwalking again, is she?"

"Oh, no! Or not that I know of! I was looking for you."

"And since when have I been in the habit of sleeping downstairs?" Matron demanded.

"Oh, I know. The thing is I came to report that the radiator in Pansy isn't working and the dormitory's like an icehouse. I did go to your room, but you weren't there, so I thought you might have found it out yourself and gone down to see if the furnaces were all right. When I couldn't find you there, I was coming back; only I tripped on the end of my blanket and dropped my torch," Len explained.

The wrath died as Matron replied, "I see. I was in Gentian. Primrose Trevoase woke up with violent toothache and came to see me for something to relieve it. What is this about the radiators? Come back to your dormitory and let me see. Lift that end or you'll be tripping up again."

"Should I go and find my torch first?" Len asked meekly.

"No; I'll see to it presently. You come with me and don't go on trying to wake up the entire school." And Matron led the way up the second flight of stairs into the upper corridor. They passed one of the radiators there and Matron touched it as they passed. She exclaimed. "Cold as charity! What has Gaudenz been doing?"

"I don't think it's the furnaces. I went into the boiler room and they seemed all right as far as I could see."

"Did you open any of the doors?"

"No; I didn't exactly like to."

"Good! We don't want a fire at this time of night!" With which they reached Pansy and as Matron entered, she gave a shiver. "You were quite right to come for me! This place is like a refrigerator! Keep that blanket round you."

"It woke me, it was so cold. And it woke Jack Lambert, too. The rest were asleep when I left," Len explained.

"That's more than they are now." Matron switched on the lights. "Keep right under the bedclothes, all of you. Now, Len, which is Jack's cubicle?"

"This one!" Len led the way and pulled the curtains aside. Matron marched in. There was no visible sign of Jack. No black head lay on the pillow. But at the foot of the bed, the plumeau was slightly humped up. Matron bent over and hauled everything back, exhibiting Jack, cowering at the foot of the bed. Her eyes were screwed tightly shut and her fingers were in her ears.

She removed them with a jerk as the cold air struck her and gave a squawk. "Go away! I'm not a bit afraid of you and if you touch me I'll yell blue murder! Go away, or I'll yell! Help—"

She got no further, for Matron smothered the yell at birth.

"Bless my soul!" she said blankly. "What nonsense is this? Come up to your proper place in the bed and stop talking rubbish! Quiet, everyone!" as her quick ears caught rustles and gasps. "I will not have the whole school wakened if I can help it! Now, Jack! Up you come!"

Like it or not, up Jack came! Matron might be small, but she was very wiry. She had the writhing Jack up on her pillow and the clothes tucked firmly round her before that young woman had recovered from the shock of being firmly gagged by a small hand placed over her mouth. Len put the finishing touch.

"Jack, you utter idiot! Pipe down! It's Matron and me! What's wrong with you?"

Jack opened one eye to survey them. Reassured, she opened the other to stare.

"Gosh! I thought it was burglars breaking in!"

"What on earth are you talking about?" Matron demanded trenchantly.

"Well—it was all quiet—and then there was a terrific crash and sounds like someone hammering and—and I thought they were smashing their way in."

Len grinned. "That was my torch. Anyhow, burglars don't break in anywhere with a din of that kind. It wouldn't pay them!"

"Apart from which," Matron added, "perhaps you would tell me just what a school would be likely to contain that would attract burglars? Have you taken leave of your senses, child?"

The badly crushed Jack had no more to say.

"Now," Matron said, raising her voice so that everyone else could hear, "this dormitory is cold. Something seems to have happened to the radiator. Len is coming with me to fetch extra blankets and I will bring you each a drink of hot milk. After that, you may all lie down and go to sleep again. In the meanwhile, everyone is to lie down and keep right under the bedclothes. Come along, Len. I'll give you blankets and you can begin to put them over the beds while I see to the milk. No talking, anyone!"

She marched Len off and the Junior Middles, left alone, had to lie there in silence. Needless to state, every last one of them was nearly bursting with curiosity—except Jack. She was still too ashamed of the scene she had made for that.

31

Presently Len came staggering back under a pile of fluffy blankets. Matron came a little later with another pile before she went off to find out how many more of the girls had been roused by Len's exploits or the cold. All the dormitories on the top floor were suffering, but so far everyone seemed to be sound asleep except the members of Pansy. Satisfied, Matron returned to her milk which was nearly boiling by this time. She filled beakers and arrived in Pansy with a steaming trayful. Len had an extra blanket on every bed by that time, her own included, and the hot milk finished what they had begun. By the time the last empty beaker had been returned, the Middles were turning drowsy. Len was ordered back to bed and Matron, who had taken time to don a few clothes against the bitter cold, returned to her own room where she switched on the fire and sipped a beaker of milk on her own account while she laid her plans.

"There must be an airlock somewhere," she thought. "We can't tackle that now. Gaudenz must see to it in the morning. Meanwhile, those youngsters should be warm enough by this time. I must do something about the others though. I do not intend to have an epidemic of sniffles at this date! I'll have to have help. She finished her milk. "That's better! I feel warm again. Now who—Ah! Kathie Ferrars and Nancy Wilmot sleep at this end of the staff corridor. I'll call them and they can help me. First to get out the blankets, though!"

By the time she had got enough blankets to give one extra to each bed on the top storey, she was warm indeed. She carried as many as she could upstairs, called in at Pansy where she found everyone sleeping peacefully, and then made for the corridor where the staff bedrooms were.

Matron roused her two colleagues, told them what was wrong and bade them come and help her spread extra blankets in all the dormitories affected.

"How has it happened, Matey?" Miss Ferrars asked as she hurriedly pulled on a few warm clothes.

"I've no idea. Gaudenz must see to it in the morning. But those radiators are as cold as stone and the dormitories are regular icehouses," Matron said, borrowing Len's description. "I don't want to rouse anyone if it can be helped. Your job is to help me lay an extra blanket over each bed without waking the girls."

"We'll never do it!" Nancy Wilmot declared. "Someone is bound to wake up and yell. We'd better be prepared to smother anyone likely to raise the roof. Ready, Kathy? Come on, then! But prepare for the worst, I warn you both!"

How they ever did it without waking at least half the girls, none of them ever knew. As it turned out, the only people to rouse, and they not fully, were Con Maynard who turned over and murmured something; Betty Landon, who had to be efficiently smothered by the watchful Miss Wilmot; and Richenda Fry, who grappled with Matron and nearly succeeded in throttling her. By the time they had calmed Richenda down, the mistresses were nearly choking with suppressed giggles. It was after three before everyone was safely in bed again, but, thanks to the measures she had taken, Matron had the satisfaction of knowing that not a girl was any the worse for what Len, describing it to her mother later, called "The Big Freeze".

Gaudenz found the airlock next morning and set things right, but when the corridors began to warm up and the frozen radiators to thaw, it was plain that the frost had left trouble behind it. Trickles of water appeared on the floors and there was a good time had by all before finally those wretched things could be got to work again.

Still, as Arda remarked, it made a good story for their home letters and Pansy had scored over the rest by hot milk in the middle of the night, so it might have been much worse!

Chapter 4

JACK HAS AN IDEA

THANKS to that episode, Jack forgot the questions with which she had meant to ply Len and gave her dormitory prefect a rest for nearly a week. Len was thankful for it. She was an unselfish creature and she had done her best to satisfy Jack's perpetual curiosity, but, as she herself said, it got monotonous after a while.

"That wretched infant seems to think I'm a travelling encyclopedia," she had complained to her chum, Ted Grantley. "Half the time I have to tell her to wait and then I have to go fishing for an answer—of sorts, anyhow. I've quite enough on my plate without adding to it like that!"

This was on the Saturday afternoon following the eventful night. Va and b were all in the Senior common room taking their ease. It was their turn to entertain the school that evening. Everything was ready now and they felt entitled to sit back and relax.

Con laughed. "She caught me yesterday when you weren't available, Len, and asked why Margot's eye was going all the colours of the rainbow and was it just like any ordinary bruise?"

"What did you tell her?" Margot demanded.

"Said a bruise was a bruise, wherever you got it. I must say, Margot, that was a nasty bang you gave yourself."

Margot, whose eye was now free from swelling though the area round it was still at the colourful stage, giggled. "That wasn't the word for it! Talk of seeing stars! I saw three galaxies at once! Mary-Lou was in this morning and she ran into me in the entrance hall and had a good old stare at it. She said they'd been rather at their wits' end about it as you couldn't have a Fairy Queen in any panto who looked as if she'd been in a free fight and there wasn't another soul who could manage those frightfully high notes in that solo Plato's given her. It's the outside edge! I go right up to E in alt—high E, then!" as Ricki Fry goggled at her. "Plato must have been crackers when he composed that! However, as I pointed out, the panto doesn't come of till the end of the month which gives me another three weeks to get rid of the bruise."

Every Easter term, St. Mildred's, the finishing branch of the Chalet School, gave a pantomime for the benefit of all dwellers on the Görnetz Platz and the shelves near at hand. The proceeds went to the big Sanatorium at the far end of the Platz, to help with the free wards. It was an annual event anticipated with lively pleasure each year. The "Millies" wrote the book and the lyrics themselves, and for music either "lifted" well-known airs or applied to the school's somewhat eccentric singing master. The school helped with the orchestra and usherettes and other attendants. Usually, St. Mildred's supplied most of the main characters in the cast but, in case of need, it was understood that they could draw on the school proper.

This year, they had decided on *Snow White and the Seven Dwarfs* for their story. This meant that they had to have a Snow White who could be carried easily, which, in turn, had meant Verity Carey, sister-by-marriage of the said Mary-Lou, who was built on a miniature scale. Verity, the owner of a sweet mezzo-soprano, had been their Fairy Queen for the past three or four years, so that meant looking for someone else to take the part. They pitched on Margot Maynard, who was not only a lovely girl but possessed what promised to become a true dramatic soprano, full and sweet and of no little power. All the Maynards sang, from the doctor and Mrs. Maynard—who had herself been the school's prima donna for many years —down to three-year-old Cecil, who already had a very true little treble. Margot, however, looked like becoming outstanding and already Joey

Maynard had talked to Mr. Denny about having her voice properly trained when she was a little older.

"Are you going to take up singing when you leave school?" Rosamund Lilley asked.

Margot flushed and shook her head. "I don't think so—not specially, anyhow."

"It's a waste if you don't," Jo Scott, form prefect of Va, remarked severely.

"I'm all out for a quiet life!" Margot retorted. "Concert work would be too much like hard work."

"Then what are you going to do?" Betty Landon asked with curiosity. "You've never said yet, though most of the rest of us have some idea by this time. Len's going to teach and Con means to write. Rosamund is taking up horticulture and Ricki is going tooth and nail for curios and old china. Even *I* know now what I'm going to do, though I swithered over it when I found out all it meant."

"What are you going to do?" Len demanded quickly.

"PT—if I can get into one of the training colleges. But never mind me! I want to know what's Margot's idea. Come on, Margot!"

Margot was pink again, rather to the amazement of the rest, but she held up her head. "I can't be absolutely sure—yet. I rather think it may be something to do with teaching—and singing; but I don't know yet. Nothing's decided and I can't tell you. Stop teasing, Betty!"

Betty's eyes were wide with curiosity. She was noted in the school for being inquisitive. Len pitched in quickly, for Margot was looking upset.

"My goodness, Betty! What on earth's set you, of all people, on to PT? You'll have to work a jolly sight harder at science and chemmy and all that sort of thing if that's your idea!"

"I know!" Betty heaved a deep sigh. "It's a sickening nuisance that they want all that theoretical work as well as games and gym; but there you are! I've quite decided, so I'll have to pull up my socks and hoe in at the lot, worse luck!"

"Shock for Bill when it does happen!" someone remarked with a chuckle. "Do you think she'll survive it, anyone?"

It was Betty's turn to blush. So far, she had restricted her efforts at lessons to the minimum which would keep her out of serious trouble. If she began to take a real interest in her work it would certainly create a minor sensation!

Her friend, Alicia Leonard, came to her rescue. "Most of us seem to be on the hoeing-in side this year. Do you folk realise that most of us are sixteen or very nearly sixteen? We'll have two more years at school at most and then we'll start on our careers."

"Oxford for me at eighteen!" Len cried. "I'll have three years there and then I'm trying for a job in some school or other."

"You'll get a job here for the asking," big Joan Baker, the eldest of them, said abruptly.

"No thank you! Oh, I hope I shall come back to teach —but not until all the kids that have been at school with me have grown up and left!" Len said decidedly.

The talk turned to their plans for the evening and the question of Margot's future career was shelved.

The first three days of that week had been fine with only an occasional flurry of snow and that mostly at night. On the Thursday the school wakened to find the grey skies turning yellowish and then black, and by the afternoon the snow had come in earnest. So had the wind, hurling itself down from the north, howling round the school buildings in the eeriest manner, and piling up great drifts all round. The girls had been prisoners ever since, for in such a blizzard as this no one was allowed to go outside. Mary-Lou had only reached the school that morning by grace of one of the doctors from the Sanatorium, who had brought her in his car and taken her back when she had concluded her interview with Miss Annersley.

Staff and girls had sighed resignedly and buckled down to work, knowing that when the weather cleared again, they would have extra time off for open air sports and walks. The elder girls were contented enough, but the younger ones had reached their limits by the time Saturday afternoon came, and were ripe for any mischief that came along.

"I'm sick of the house!" Jack grumbled. "When's this beastly snow going to stop? It's been going for ages!"

"When it feels like it," Arda told her. "And 'beastly' is a forbidden word. If any of the prees or the mistresses hear you, you'll be fined."

"Well, it is beastly and there's no other word for it!" Jack retorted.

"It's no worse for you than for anyone else," Margaret Twiss told her sharply. "You pipe down! You're a new girl and new girls sing very small their first term."

"That's rot!" Rosemary Wentworth cried. "It depends on the new girls. Anyhow, you were new yourself last term! I never noticed that you piped down if you thought you could get away with it. Pipe down now, yourself!"

As Rosemary had been at the school for more than two years, Margaret felt it better to say no more, though if looks could have killed, the glare she treated Rosemary to would have stretched that young woman flat on the floor on the spot!

"I agree with Jack," Angèle Sartou, who came from the south of France, observed. "Me, I like snow very well, but not when it goes on and on and on as it does now. And the wind—how it howls! Like wolves that range themselves in search of prey!"

"We don't have wolves up here," Renata pointed out in a matter-of-fact way. "I don't believe there are any in Switzerland—not wild ones."

But Angèle's dramatics had started something. "Wouldn't it be awful if, when the snow stops, we couldn't open the doors?" Caroline Smith suggested.

"Whatever would they do?" Jack asked. "They don't open outward anywhere, do they? None that I've seen, anyhow."

Arda giggled. "Do you think the snow would fall in on top of whoever did open the door?" she asked. "And if they don't have wolves here they do have bears. I've read about it in a book my grandmother had when she was a little girl. Perhaps some bears are pr-r-rowling round the house this very moment."

It is impossible to give a real idea of the eeriness in Arda's accent as she rolled her R's, but it set quite half the other youngsters jumping. Rosemary, who was the form prefect, felt dimly that she ought to stop this or some of them would be shrieking before you knew where you were. She changed the conversation.

"Who d'you think would be the first to open an outer door?" she asked. "The Head—or no; Deney, most likely."

"Or p'r'aps Matey," Barbara Hewlett suggested. "It would come with a wallop, whoever it was!" She giggled whole-heartedly. "Oh wouldn't she be mad!"

Jack's eyes were gleaming. "Let's go and pull open one of the side doors and see what happens!" she proposed wickedly.

She was instantly suppressed by everyone.

"But no! Certainly not!" Yolande le Cadoulec, niece of a former Chalet School girl, cried emphatically. "We should be in the most terrible trouble!"

As she spoke in her native French, Jack was not much wiser. However, Rosemary, using her common sense, grabbed at her as she made an impetuous dive for the door, all set to carry out her sinful idea.

"No you don't!" Rosemary exclaimed, holding her tightly. "D'you know what it'd mean? They'd never let us be alone again for a single afternoon. D'you want us to have a pree or a mistress stuck in with us like the kids all the time?"

Decidedly Jack did not. She had been at school long enough to realise something of the joy of their freedom from supervision during their free periods.

"We might just open it a chink," she tempted. "There wouldn't be much snow could get in then. Oh, do let's!"

"No fear! Not the teeniest chink of a chink!" Rosemary proclaimed. "You mayn't mind getting into a row, but we do! Pipe down, Jack, and don't be such an idiot!"

Jack looked round them all, but no one was with her. "You're not going to do it," Rosemary insisted. "Have you forgotten that it's the Fifth's Evening tonight? Matey would bang the lot of us off to bed and we'd miss the whole thing. It's safe to be something jolly good. That crowd have brains and I'll bet they've thought up something jolly worthwhile! You leave the outer doors alone. Let's play—let's play rhyming charades! Come on! You pick up for one side, Wanda, and I'll pick up for the others. Bags me first pick! Jack Lambert!"

Jack went to her side and as Wanda instantly called Renata to her, the two worst scamps in Lower IIIa were safely corralled for the time being.

"The snow'll be there tomorrow all right," Jack thought as she peered through the top of the windows to see if she could find out if it had stopped. It was pitch black outside, for they had the lights on. She gave it up and turned her attention to the charades, which kept them all occupied for the rest of the afternoon.

When Kaffee und Kuchen was ending, Josette Russell stood up and told them to clear the tables as fast as they could and then hurry off upstairs and change into their evening velveteens, also as fast as they could, and come straight down to Hall.

"Bring cardigans with you," she finished. "I don't know what the programme is, but Jo Scott tells me it isn't dancing or games, and even with the central heating you may feel cold if you're just sitting. Now that's all. Finish the meal and get down to it!"

She exchanged a grin with Jo before she sat down again, and after that there was no delay. Everyone finished quickly and ten minutes later the tables were cleared and they were all upstairs, changing out of their school frocks into the gentian blue velveteens with muslin collars and cuffs which constituted their usual evening wear in winter.

Out in the corridors, the school prefects took them in charge and they were marched down to Hall in due order.

The long green forms were standing in rows as usual, but the curtains which were usually drawn up to the sides had been let down and pulled close. The concert grand had been shifted from the dais to the floor in front and cushions for the Juniors and wicker chairs for the staff had been set in front of the forms.

"Play!" Rosemary murmured delightedly. "Oh, scrummy!"

"Or those word charades—or tableaux," Barbara chimed in. "Shove up, Jack! You don't want all that much room! Come on, Renata and Arda! Heaps of room here for you!"

Just what the two senior Fifths were going to do with them remained to be seen, but they were all sure it would be something delightful. Even Jack, who had been meditating on the possibility of slipping away from the rest when bedtime came and trying what would happen if you opened an outer door "just the teeniest crack," let it go for the time being, and gave her whole mind to lawful joys—for the time being, anyhow.

Chapter 5

A THRILLING EVENING

PROMPTLY on the chime of seventeen-hours-thirty from the big school clock, the curtains parted and Len Maynard in her velveteen frock appeared before them. At the same moment, the footlights went up and all other lights in the Hall were switched off with stunning suddenness.

"Good evening, school!" Len began. "Can you all hear me?"

They assured her that they could. Her clear, beautifully modulated voice had the same trick of carrying which the Head's had.

"I won't keep you for more than a minute or two," she continued with a beaming smile. "First of all, we are presenting a series of scenes from various well-known books. We are miming the scenes and we want you to guess to what book each belongs. In a moment you will have cards and pencils given out to you so that you can write down the titles. In between the scenes, some of us will entertain you with music."

She paused for a moment and the school began to clap. She held up her hand for silence and the mistresses hushed everyone vigorously. They wanted to hear what else she had to say.

"I haven't quite finished," she remarked. "First of all, we ask that no one will so much as whisper the name of any book she pitches on. Anyone who does will be requested to leave the Hall." Another pause. Then she added with deep meaning: Matron will go with her."

A concerted gasp from the members of the lower forms answered this. There was no need for her to explain which matron she meant. As Matron Henschell, herself an Old Girl of the school, had once remarked pensively, "She'll always be 'Matron'. The rest of us are lucky to be known as 'Matron So-and-So!'"

Len let them recover from this before she made her final observations. "We are offering a prize in each division of the school for the best list—and that includes the staff as well. That is all."

She swept them a low curtsy and vanished, followed by laughter and clapping. Not that there was much time for that, for six members of Vb, headed by Priscilla Dawbarn, arrived to distribute the cards with pencils attached. At almost the same moment Carmela Walther from Va appeared at the piano and played with considerable verve Chopin's 'Polonaise in A Major'.

She bowed gravely in thanks for the clapping that rose when she ended. Then she slithered past the row of Juniors squatting on their cushions and fled to take her place backstage. Half a minute later, a bell rang and the curtains were drawn back to reveal what looked, as little Sharlie Andrews, the Junior English mistress, described as "A glory-hole if ever there was one!"

The Fifth forms had contented themselves with the black curtains that were easily managed. Scenery would have taken too long. The scene was obviously an attic. Broken furniture was piled up at the back; trunks were built up in the centre; a pile of sacks lay beside them; other oddments were scattered about in untidy heaps. One of the windows from the acting cupboard had been clipped to a pair of stepladders and the curtains pinned round them. A light shone from one side and a nondescript stuffed animal was sitting on the floor.

A tall, very stout woman appeared with a boy who came up to her shoulder, though the girls had done their best to suggest his extreme youth by dressing him in a tunic, belted somewhere round his knees and ankle socks. Briony Quest's hair was closely bobbed and they had brushed up the front into an old-fashioned "toppin" which

43

they had pinned firmly. The grim-looking lady marched him in front of the trunks and produced three enormous pieces of cardboard on each of which was printed a letter —A—T—C. These she put into his hands, admonished him by shaking first her forefinger and then her head at him, and finally swept out, leaving him with the cards.

He stood staring at them. Then he set them up on one of the trunks, leaning them against the one on top, which he carefully pushed back to make a ledge. That done, he kept changing their places, every time forming no known word. Finally, he seemed to burst into tears, left them at C—T—A, grabbed the animal and pointed to his latest effort before lying down in the beam of light and going to sleep. The curtain fell, and everyone was laughing and applauding. *Das Buch von Trott* was a favourite with the girls and even the Second formers knew it. Only Jack remained blankly ignorant.

The next scene was another she did not know, though it was the meeting of the Pickwick Club, taken from that hoary favourite, *Little Women*. For the first time in her life she wished that she had read a little more. However, the next one gave her plenty of company, for it proved a real teaser.

It was plain that this was a schoolroom, for forms were set across one side at an angle and a blackboard stood opposite.

Centre back was a gentleman with a book. Round him stood half a dozen people. On the front form sat Len Maynard, her hair done in two pigtails, dropping over her shoulders while she and the rest of the boys and girls sitting in the forms all seemed to be working hard. Suddenly the "boy" sitting next to Len picked up one pigtail with a grin, seemed to say something, and she jumped up, glaring at him. Then she slammed him over the head with her cardboard—they had been unable to obtain slates —and the rest of the pupils made gestures of horror and dismay. The schoolmaster left his class, came forward and took her by the shoulder, marching her to the blackboard where he stood her, pretending to write something on it—if he had written the actual words, the title would have been given away—and then walked back to his class which he called to order with a sharp gesture. Everyone else fell to work again and the curtain fell with Len in her prominent position wearing the look of a martyr.

The school applauded, but there were a good many puzzled faces and most people wrote down nothing, though one or two of the staff managed a title.

"I know it," Josette muttered to her next-door neighbour, Clare Kennedy, "but I'll be sugared if I can put a name to it! What on earth is it?"

"No use asking me; I haven't a clue," Clare returned. "I know it all right, but I can't place it."

However, the next scene came from the charming Swiss story, *Heidi*, and even Jack knew this—almost the only one she did know. Then came the courting by the Lunatic Gentleman of Mrs. Nickleby out of *Nicholas Nickleby*, which brought peals of laughter from everyone. The curtains fell amidst shrieks of laughter which lasted until Len, her hair in its usual long curly tail, appeared before the audience once more to announce that there would now be an interval for Abendessen.

"By kind permission of Miss Annersley," she said primly, "Prayers will not take place until the Evening is ended. We are having a twenty minutes' interval and I know you will be pleased to hear that we are to leave clearing the tables till later. Will you please not loiter over your meal as we have several more scenes for you."

Then she scuttled off and Carmela, who had gone to the piano again, struck up a march and the school instantly marched out to the Speisesaal.

Jack was having as good a time as anyone though, as she complained to Renata, it was hard lines on her not knowing the books. She had no chance of a prize!

"Well, you'd better do some reading," Barbara Hewlett, who had overheard her, remarked. "We shall

45

have this again, sometime—with different books, of course."

Jack made a face, but said no more, though she had already decided that this was something she must do. "I'll bet Anne's got most of them," she thought. "She's always got her nose in a book when she's at home!"

Back in the Hall, the audience settled itself in a pleasing state of anticipation. What would come next?

What came next was a complete mystery to practically everyone. The stage was empty, except for some tall jars of pampas grass from the art room which had been set on either side. Between these appeared a procession. First came a heavily bearded man wearing a rakish hat. On his arm was a lady in a long, full dress with a sun-bonnet shielding her face. After them came two boys drawing an animal composed of two other people who represented an ass. On the ass's back, leaning against a bundle, was Renée Touvet, the smallest member of the two forms and also dressed as a boy. Last of all came a youth who loitered behind and kept looking from side to side. He carried a blackboard ruler over his shoulder. Suddenly he stopped, levelled the ruler at the grass and was clearly shooting something. Then he ran to the side while the others stopped to watch. At last he took off his coat, threw it over the creature which had figured in the first scene and brought it to exhibit to the others. After everyone had clearly praised him, it was put on the ass's back, whereupon that intelligent beast began to kick its hind legs and toss its head, finally gallumphing off.

"What on earth—" Miss Derwent, who taught Senior English, gasped.

"No use asking me, my love!" Miss Wilmot retorted. "It's got me completely guessing. This particular scene is going to be a blank on my card!"

It looked like being a blank on everyone's card until Jack suddenly gave a loud whoop and scribbled on hers. Later, Kathy Ferrars picked it up and showed it with appreciative giggles to the rest. "Swiss Famerly

Robbinson" was written. Spelling was not Jack's strong point!

"I must say," said the Head, mopping her eyes—the ass's gyrations had been funny beyond words—"that the girls have done us proud! This is most original!"

"I wonder who was responsible for it?" Matron murmured.

There was no time for a reply, for Len appeared once more to announce that, as the next scene would take a little time to arrange, they were to have a short sing-song. Carmela was already at the piano and she struck up "Röslein auf der Heiden", in which everyone joined. Other songs followed until the lights, which had been switched on during the singing, went off and the footlights blazed again. Carmela caught up her music and fled backstage and the curtains rose once more.

This was a snow scene. The stage was covered with white and certain humps were white also. And this brought an entirely unrehearsed effect, for Matron, looking at it with horror, ejaculated loudly, "Their clean sheets! The naughty girls! What next, I'd like to know?"

What next—and she gasped loudly—was the arrival of the hand trolley Gaudenz used for moving the trunks at the beginning and end of term. It was pushed through the curtains by a figure clad in a long cloak and a beret. She made for a patch of shadow and hauled out with a distinct rumpling of the sheets a queer creature attired in a torn shirt and trousers with bare legs and feet which were dyed scarlet! (Francie Wilford had used a whole bottle of red ink to get this effect.)

At this moment, a party of boys and girls appeared, carrying armfuls of vegetables begged from the kitchen. At the sight of the man's discovery, they dropped the lot and ran to him and among them carried his find backstage, leaving trolley, vegetables and badly crumpled sheets for the curtains to descend on.

The school applauded frantically, partly because a good many of them recognised the book, but also because the

Fifths had had the nerve to use their sheets and had given Matron a shock!

The next was easy enough, for it was the famous scene from *Oliver Twist* where Oliver asks for more. It was slightly diversified by the Matron tripping up over a forgotten onion and nearly falling headlong on top of the form where half a dozen untidy-looking objects sat before their bowls.

The final one proved the worst of the lot to guess. In the centre of the stage was the ass, drawing the trolley for a change, with a man sitting on the extreme edge of the trolley, holding the string reins by which the animal was tethered.

Round the corner of the curtain appeared two young ladies with ringlets bobbing under their poke bonnets, wearing ankle-length gowns and shawls. Next appeared two elderly ladies, with sidecurls. The young ladies curtsied and were kissed. A large volume was put in the hands of each and they made their way to their remarkable equipage where the taller one climbed up. The shorter looked down at her tome, ran back and pushed it into the hands of the thin lady before hurrying to scramble into the narrow space left by her companion. The ass, with a mighty effort, got its burden moving and they trundled off in a series of jerks that bade fair to unseat every one of the party, and the curtain fell for the last time.

The audience clapped vociferously and then Len appeared, grinning broadly. She held up her hand for silence and when she got it, she beamed round on everyone and said, "That's the lot. Someone please switch on the lights and then you can correct and we'll see who has won the prizes. I'm going to read the titles out in turn."

Josette jumped up and ran to the switches and when she was back in her seat, Len proceeded to read out the list of book titles.

"Scene I is from *Das Buch von Trott*, where Trott tries

48

to spell CAT. Scene II comes from *Little Women*. It was the meeting of Pickwick Club. Scene III." Here, she stopped and grinned. She had heard one or two comments during Abendessen. "Aren't you all slow? That was from *Anne of Green Gables*—the scene where Gilbert calls Anne's hair 'carrots' and she breaks her slate over his head."

"I knew I knew it!" Josette proclaimed in clarion tones. "How I could have forgotten, I shall never know!"

Len gave her cousin a grin before she proceeded. "Scene IV was from *Heidi* where Heidi goes to town for the first time. And you all must have guessed the *Nicholas Nickleby* scene. Scene VI was *The Swiss Family Robinson*—you remember; where Fritz shoots the porcupine and when they put it on the donkey's back, the quills stick in and the donkey bolts with Franz."

"Scene VII is from *Sans Famille* where the gardener and his family find Rémi nearly dead in the snow. Scene VIII was *Oliver Twist*, of course. And the last scene is *Vanity Fair*—where Becky Sharp and Amelia Sedley leave the Miss Pinkerton's seminary. That's all. Will you please count up.'

No one had guessed all the scenes, but Anna Hoffman of VIb had named six of them correctly and got the prize for the Seniors. The Senior Middles' went to Janice Chester of Upper IVb who was reputed to read everything that came her way and who had seven titles on her list. The Junior Middles' was won by Sally Godfrey from Lower IVb, and in the Juniors, the prize fell to Anne de Guitry, a small French girl whose mother was half-English and who had seen to it that Anne knew English storybooks as well as French ones. The prizes were boxes of sweets which the two forms had clubbed together to fill from their own supplies of tuck.

Among the staff, Miss Derwent had beaten the rest with seven titles and was presented with a pincushion in the form of a flower which Jeanne Daudet had spent the afternoon in making.

After that, they had Prayers and then everyone but the prefects was marched off to bed. Matron said nothing about the sheets that night, but she went the rounds next day and those members of the Fifths who had sacrificed themselves heard all about it!

Chapter 6

JACK IN TROUBLE

THE snow continued all Sunday. Monday was no better and it was still snowing hard when they got up on Tuesday morning. By this time, the drifts had almost covered the downstairs windows. The lights had burned downstairs continuously throughout the five days, but it was possible to look out of the dormitory windows and behold a bleak white desert which had once been the garden.

"Coo! Isn't the place changed!" Jack commented that morning when she, with the rest of Pansy, was engaged in dormitory chores. "You'd never think there were bushes all over the shop!"

"French, please," came automatically from Len's cubicle. She suddenly appeared and bore down on Jack. "This is French day, Jack. Come along; I'll help you. Repeat after me—'Ma foi! Que tout est changé!'"

Very reluctantly Jack repeated the French after Len. "It's a jolly nuisance!" she grumbled. "Why can't we just say it?"

"Because one of the reasons why you are here is to help you to learn to speak both French and German fluently and easily," Len told her.

Somehow, everything went wrong with Jack that day. She had made a complete mess of her arithmetic home-work and it was returned in consequence. She had done her French exercise very carelessly, neglecting the fact that in French, adjectives agree with their nouns in gender and number. Result: another returned lesson and a few pointed remarks from Mlle.

During Break, someone turning unexpectedly caught

51

her arm, and her frock was deluged with cocoa that was quite hot enough to be unpleasant. There was no help for it. Jack must change, for she was soaked to the skin. Barbara Chester, who was on duty, told José Helston exactly what she thought of her before marching the pair of them off to Matron. By the time she had finished with José, that young woman was exceedingly sorry for herself. Jack came in for the backwash, Matron remarking that she should have kept her eyes open and not allowed José to jog her arm. By the time it was all over and Jack was in her Sunday skirt and a jumper, Break had come to an end and she had missed practically the whole of it.

It was a mercy that the lesson immediately after was geography, which she liked. Miss Bertram improved matters by giving them a lesson on the way in which the relief of a country affected the population. Before ten minutes were over, the entire form was eagerly using the synthetic maps she had borrowed for them from Inter V and when, at the end, she collected the said maps, everyone backed up Barbara Hewlett's urgent request that they might have synthetic maps of their own. Miss Bertram laughed and promised to see what the stockroom could spare before she took her departure.

By this time, Jack's face had cleared and she was her usual cheerful self. Unfortunately, it didn't last. The next lesson was English dictation. When Miss Andrews corrected their work, she expressed her horror at the twenty-one mistakes Jack had managed in about twelve lines of dictation.. For jolly little Miss Andrews, she was positively scathing and Jack, faced with those twenty-one words to write out six times each instead of the normal three on top of two returned lessons, felt that life was using her very hardly. All her other grievances returned in a flood and she sulked for the rest of the morning; she sulked throughout Mittagessen; during their rest period she sat and gloomed at her book without turning a single page. She folded up her chair at the end with all the noise she could contrive. And in gym, she disobeyed a direct command from Miss Burnett to come down from the ribstalls and wait to climb until the mats were in position. Instead of coming down, she went up and had to be lifted down. Peggy Burnett was an easy-going person, but even she would not put up with this sort of thing. She had a sharp tongue when she was roused and by the time Jack was dismissed from the gym with orders to go to her form room and write out twenty times in her best handwriting, "In gymnastics, I must obey on the word and without argument", her ears were tingling and she also had the unpleasant knowledge that she had two order-marks to give in at the end of the afternoon. One more, and she must miss next Saturday's Evening and do sewing for Matron instead.

Needlework, which was Jack's bugbear, rounded off the lessons for the afternoon and once more she found herself outside the door before ten minutes were over. At fifteen-thirty, when the rest of the form returned to the formroom for half-an-hour's prep before the end of school, Jack had to go back and explain to Mlle—if she could—just why she had been so rude and tiresome. By this time, she was boiling with rage and she answered Mlle's strictures with downright impertinence, adding to her sins by speaking in English.

By the time Mlle had finished, however, all impertinence had vanished. What she had to say took all the starch out of Jack—especially when she was condemned to an hour's sewing after evening prep to make up for the time she had lost in the afternoon.

She got through the evening somehow, including the sewing which she had to do sitting beside Mlle as she gave a French reading to the members of the two Sixths. It was Greek to Jack and she simply hated being there with all the big girls and having to sew carefully with neat, even stitches at the hem of a petticoat for herself. The Chalet School believed in teaching old-fashioned plain sewing in the lower forms.

She refused to speak to anyone for the short time that

53

was left between Abendessen and bed, and the rest, warned by her black scowl, sheered off and left her to herself. Jack felt ill-used over that, but if anyone had tried to talk to her, the chances are that she would have been given a nasty snub. Len Maynard, encountering her in one of the corridors, saw the look on her face and wondered. Jack stalked past her without any notice and this was so unlike Jack that Len knew something was wrong. Being a responsible young person, she vowed to get to the bottom of it as soon as she could, but until the Junior Middles went up to bed, she had no chance. Then she conveniently remembered that she had meant to get a clean handkerchief. It was true that she herself would be going to bed in an hour's time, but she must do something about Jack Lambert, and her handkerchief was a good excuse.

She left the common room and went to hunt up someone to ask permission. She ran straight into Miss Andrews.

"May I go up to my dormitory to get a clean handkerchief, please?" she asked in her fluent, pretty French.

"Certainly," Miss Andrews said. Then she laughed. "But it is not like you, Len, to forget such a thing. Yes, go by all means."

Thanking her, Len went flying up the stairs in a way that would have brought her a smart reproof from anyone in authority if she had been caught. However, no one was about.

Len went to find her handkerchief first. She could hear sounds from the other cubicles, indicating that her juniors were getting ready for bed. They were doing it with reasonable speed and order, so she said nothing. But just as she reached Jack's cubicle, she heard that young person getting into bed and, judging by the noise, she had tossed herself down with all the vim of which she was capable.

Len went to look in on Jack. There was little to be seen of her but a cropped black head just above the bedclothes. She dropped the curtains and walked up to the bed where she sat down on the edge in direct defiance of rules. Jack promptly pushed down the bedclothes and turned to look.

"Well," Len said, speaking in English, since the day was practically over for Jack and it would be quicker, "what's gone wrong with you? Hurry up and tell me, for I shouldn't be here; but I'm not letting any one of you kids look as you've done all today without finding out what's up."

"Nothing's wrong, only things is all colleywest with me!" Jack growled, using a home colloquialism that she had been strictly forbidden to use. Her home was in Cheshire and the Cheshire dialect is not very pretty.

"*What*?" exclaimed Len, startled by the unknown expression.

"I said things is all colleywest with me—and so they are! Nothing but fusses from morning till night! I'm sick of it!"

"Oh, it's like that, is it?" Len ruminated a moment or two. Then she stooped down to pull up the blankets and tuck them in more securely. "Well, there isn't time to talk about it just now. It'll be Lights Out for you folk in two minutes. You forget it and go to sleep. Tomorrow is also a day, as the Spanish say. Most likely it'll be quite different and things won't be—whatever it was you said."

"Well, it won't then. I've done scarcely anything at my prep—too many returned lessons!" Jack retorted.

"Hard luck! Look, Jack, I can't talk with you now; but if you like to hurry over your getting-up in the morning and come to me in your form room, I'll do what I can to help you with your prep. Now goodnight and cheer up!"

Len patted a shoulder and left the dormitory. She also left a partly consoled Jack, who was really tired out with the day's trials and her own very mixed emotions and who soon fell alseep though she had been certain she wouldn't.

She woke up next morning remembering Len's promise, and the moment the rising-bell went, she was out of bed and stripping the bedclothes as fast as she could go. She felt better for a good night's rest and there was always the hope that the snow had stopped and they might go out. Len also remembered and when she returned from the bathroom, she called Rosamund Lilley, head of the dormitory next door, into the corridor and asked her to see to Pansy for once. Rosamund was quite willing and Jack and Len were downstairs in Lower IIIa a good quarter of an hour before bell went.

"Now," said Len briskly, "be quick and get your prep out, for you haven't a moment to lose. By the way, you haven't any practice at this time have you?"

"No; I don't learn music," Jack explained.

"Good! Now what have you to do? Arithmetic and Latin and rep? Right! What have you done anything at?"

"I learned my Latin vocab in prep, but I haven't looked at the translation. I haven't touched my sums and I'm not sure of the rep."

Len thought. "We'll leave the Latin. If you know your vocab, you ought to be able to manage some sort of translation. We'll do the arithmetic first. Show it to me and we'll see."

Jack showed the sums—three mixed fractions, none of them very difficult.

"Easy enough," Len observed. "You have to give your answers in decimals, so you know what you have to do first, don't you?"

"Make them all decimals—but I'm not sure how to do it," Jack replied.

"I'll show you and then you can go on by yourself. Look, Jack! You have 2½ to turn into a decimal. First change it to an improper fraction—you know how to do that?"

Jack knew. "Five over two," she said, looking at Len hopefully.

"Right! Now to turn it into a decimal, divide the denominator into the numerator—like this. Two into five?"

"Twice and one over," Jack said promptly.

"Write it down. Now put your point. Now imagine a nought after the one. Two into ten?"

56

"Five." Jack wrote it down. "Is that all?"

"That's all; except that in one or two of those, you may have to go on adding noughts. Get cracking and see if you can finish quickly."

With this help, Jack had no trouble. She went through those three sums like wildfire and when she had copied them into her exercise book still had ten minutes for her repetition. When the sound of the gong boomed through the building, she left her books piled up by her desk and followed Len out, feeling her usual self once more.

Her own crowd were thankful to see it. Without trying, Jack had become something of a leader among them and they had missed her cheeky cheeriness the day before. When they went upstairs again, they found that one good thing had happened. The snow had ceased falling at last!

"Scrummy!" Jack exclaimed as she looked out of the window. She raised her voice. "I say, Len!"

"Well—what? Get on with your work, Jack!" returned Len, leaving her cubicle and coming to see what was wanted.

"It's stopped snowing! When will we be let go out?"

"What ghastly English!" Len cried with a laugh. "Honestly, Jack! As for going out, I don't suppose it'll be today. The new snow will be too soft."

Jack gave it up and Len went out and thought no more of the matter. But the young monkey had been reminded of her own idea on Saturday. She was spoiling for mischief after all the sulks of the day before. What a lark it would be to pull one of the doors open and see a whole heap fall into the passage!

She fished for a clean handkerchief and found that all her handkerchiefs were out of their case and strewed everywhere in the drawer. She collected them with a grimace, but she dared not leave her drawer looking like that in case Matey should go the rounds. The quickest way was to empty the lot on her bed.

Jack proceeded to do so, and did the thing thoroughly by shaking out her handkerchief case as well. A small parcel fell out of it and she gave a smothered whoop and pocketed it on the spur of the moment. She also found a packet she had forgotten about which had been under the handkerchiefs. She stuck that into a pocket, too. Then she turned to and by the time the others were ready to leave the dormitory, the drawer was back in its place, looking immaculate.

At the Chalet School lesson time meant hard work. Jack had no chance to carry out any mischievous ideas that morning. Thanks to Len, she got through the work much better than she had ever expected and during Break Wanda and Co. kept her well occupied with their chatter. In fact, the morning went off as well as possible. Jack put her possessions away in their locker and took out her library book to change it for a fresh one, feeling as happy as ever she had been.

Miss Bertram took mid-week library. Not all the girls wanted to change their books then and it was a free period for her. On this occasion only Wanda, Renata, Margaret and a French girl, Corinne Sambeau, attended besides Jack. Renata had been reading *The Black Riders* and when she brought it, she advised Jack to snap it up.

"It is most exciting," she said. "I know you will like it, Jack."

"Oh, well, I'll take it then," Jack said, just as Margaret came to demand, "Is that *The Black Riders* you're returning, Renata? Then I'll bag it next."

"Sorry, but I've bagged it already," Jack said. She thrust herself forward, holding out the book to Miss Bertram. "Please, Miss Bertram, Renata's brought this back and may I have it next?"

"Certainly," Miss Bertram said, proceeding to cross it off Renata's page and turning to Jack's to enter it.

Margaret interfered. "Please, Miss Bertram, I said I wanted it. I've been waiting all the term for it."

Miss Bertram looked up, smiling. "I'm sorry, Margaret, but Jack spoke first. But I'll put a slip in the page saying you are to have it next," she added. "Choose something else for just now, dear, and you shall certainly have it next time."

Margaret had to give it up, but she did not love Jack any the more for her triumph.

After Rest period, during which Jack deliberately read her book at her rival, the Junior Middles has singing with Mr Denny, the school's eccentric but beloved singing-master. Jack loved singing and she sang with all her heart. Margaret was not exactly a droner, but she had a trick of going flat on high notes and was called out this afternoon and made to sing one passage by herself till she got it right. She went back to her place in no very good mood and the grin Jack gave her as she wriggled past was maddening. But English came next—grammar, too, which Jack loathed deeply. Miss Andrews was initiating them into the mysteries of analysis and she began to teach direct and indirect object today. Jack listened with perhaps half an ear and the resultant mess she made of the three sentences they were given to analyse when the actual teaching ended was enough to try anyone's temper.

Little Miss Andrews was known as one of the jolliest mistresses in the school, but she was not prepared to excuse work like this and she sent Jack back to her seat to try again with the remarks that if she couldn't do better, she had better go down to the Juniors for grammar.

"I won't accept such work from you, Jack!" she concluded. "You can do well enough when you try, but you haven't even tried with this."

Meanwhile, Margaret took up her work and received well-deserved praise for the neatness and correctness of her work.

"Oh, thank you, Miss Andrews," Margaret said, casting a triumphant glance at Jack, who happened to look up at that moment. "Please may I go and get a drink?"

"Yes; but be quick," Miss Andrews replied, turning from her to Ghislaine Touvet who had got herself into a worse muddle than Jack and now came to say despairingly that she didn't understand.

Jack didn't like Margaret any more than Margaret liked her. She was inspired at that moment to feel in her pocket for her handkerchief and she felt the tiny parcel she had popped in that morning. Oh, goody-goody! She'd show Margaret Twiss, grinning at her like that!

With Jack, to think was to act. She deliberately dropped her pencil and it rolled back to end under Margaret's chair. Up went Jack's hand to ask if she might get it. Miss Andrews, busy with Ghislaine, nodded and Jack slid down the aisle, her parcel, now unwrapped, clutched in one hand. It took her quite a minute to rescue the pencil. Then she was back in her seat and stooping absorbedly over her work when Margaret returned.

The bell rang for the end of the lesson presently and Miss Andrews, having told the form what to do for preparation, gathered her books together and stood up. At once the form stood too—and Margaret's chair came with her!

She gave a gasp and Miss Andrews stopped short.

"Good gracious, what's happened, Margaret?" she exclaimed.

"It's the chair!" Margaret gasped, pushing and struggling to free herself of it and nearly falling over in the effort. "It's stuck to me somehow! My skirt is caught!"

Miss Andrews dropped her books on the nearest desk and came to help. "Stand still, Margaret! I expect there's a loose splinter and it's caught."

But it was no loose splinter. Chair and skirt were stuck together as if they had been glued and, in the end, Margaret had to be helped out of her gym tunic. Then Miss Andrews was able to investigate properly. It took her precisely sixty seconds to solve the problem and it was a very angry Miss Andrews who stood up, faced the highly excited form and demanded in no uncertain tones, "Which of you put cobbler's wax on the seat of Margaret's chair?"

Chapter 7

WORSE AND WORSE!

A deadly silence met Miss Andrews' question. Practically everyone was staring at the mistress and Margaret. Only near the front, there was a scramble as Jack got to her feet. She might be naughty and mischievous, but she was honest.

"It was me—I mean I did it, Miss Andrews," she said.

"You!" Miss Andrews exclaimed, while the rest transferred their gaze to Jack, who had a horrid feeling that she was hemmed in by eyes and there was no escaping from them.

All the same, she stuck her chin out. She would not let that Margaret Twiss see just how stupid she was feeling—nor any of the others, for that matter. There was more than a little defiance about her attitude and Miss Andrews might be forgiven for thinking that she didn't care.

"Go and stand by my table," she said sternly. "Yolande! Aren't you in the same dormitory as Margaret?"

"But yes—in Garden," Yolande replied promptly.

"Then please go and bring her Sunday skirt down. She can't go about like that! Be quick, please! If Matron is there, you may tell her that there has been—er—an accident to Margaret's tunic and she has had to take it off."

Yolande vanished—and returned with Matron. In the meantime, Miss Andrews sent everyone but Jack to the common room. Matron swept into the room and Jack promptly wilted. Margaret herself lost her air of righteous indignation and became suddenly meek.

"What is the meaning of this?" Matron demanded while Yolande handed over the skirt to its owner.

"Jack Lambert says she put cobbler's wax on the seat of Margaret Twiss's chair and the skirt of Margaret's tunic is stuck to the chair," Miss Andrews said baldly.

"H'm! I see!" Matron turned a glare on Jack which sent the practical joker's heart down into her shoes. "And why, may I ask, did you do such a thing?"

This floored Jack completely. There was nothing she could say—or nothing that either Matron or Miss Andrews was likely to accept. She dropped the short thick lashes over her eyes and said nothing.

But if Jack was tongue-tied, Margaret was not. She was literally fuming and she burst out before anyone could stop her.

"I've never done anything to Jack to make her behave like that to me. It's her who has done things to me —bagging the library book I wanted and—and things like that! And now she's—"

She stopped there, for Matron's eyes had moved from Jack to herself and Matron's look was enough to silence a braver person than Margaret Twiss.

"I did not speak to you," Matron told her icily. She turned to Jack. "Well? I'm waiting for an answer. Why did you do it?"

"I—I—" Jack could go no further.

Matron waited a minute or two. Then, seeing that at the moment she was going to get nothing from the culprit, she acted. "Well, at least since you have done the damage, you now try to undo it. Come and work that tunic off the chair and remember, if you tear it, you will have it to mend properly in your free time."

Jack was appalled. "Matron, I—I can't!" she burst out. "It—it's cobbler's wax!"

"Well?"

"But it—it sticks—fast!"

"Oh, you did know that, did you?" This was Matron at her most awful. "And so, either to gratify some silly spite or because you thought it a clever practical joke, you chose to ruin another girl's tunic? Is that it?"

Jack had nothing to say to that.

"Or," Matron concluded, "you didn't even bother to think at all. Well, you are quite right in thinking that you could not free that skirt without tearing. I must ring up Miss Wilson and ask her advice. In the meantime you may take two order marks and come to me on Saturday for mending instead of enjoying the Evening. Also, you must pay for any repairs the tunic may need out of your pocket money. Pick up that chair and carry it to the door of my room and leave it there. Margaret, go and make yourself tidy. Go at once, both of you!"

They went without more ado. Jack was badly shaken by Matron's fiat and Margaret was swelling with indignation over the whole affir. She would jolly well see that the rest of the form knew just how nasty Jack had been to her!

What Margaret had not reckoned with was Miss Andrews. That lady had shot off to the common room where she had forbidden any of the girls to say a word to either of the pair concerned about the silly business. So when Margaret, still righteously angry, tried to speak of it to Renata, the first person she met, she got a shock.

Renata looked at her stonily and said, "Andy says we aren't to discuss it at all. And anyhow, you've been horrid to Jack ever since she came, though indeed, I don't know why. You deserved it. I'm not going to say anything else." And she turned on her heels and stalked off.

Margaret made one more effort to enlist sympathy when she had recovered from the shock this gave her. But Barbara Hewlett was even more crushing than Renata.

"I heard Renata tell you Andy said we weren't to talk about it. I'm not going to and I'm surprised you have the cheek to go on after that."

Margaret let it alone then, but it made her detest Jack even more thoroughly. She was not a favourite with anyone. She had a gift for evading her share of any blame and punishment that was going when they got into scrapes. This sort of thing does not endear a girl to anyone. It is true that Lower IIIa were rather shocked by

63

Jack's exploit but, at the same time, it struck some of the more feather-headed as very funny and all of them had realised that Margaret had taken a dislike to the new girl from the very start.

And Jack's feat seemed to have touched off a magazine. Never, in the history of the Chalet School since it had left Tirol, had there been such a series of practical jokes as were played during the next few days.

But the joke that most took the school's fancy and was added to the school's legends was one that Jack perpetrated.

She was feeling deeply injured at having to miss the Evening. She was also, like everyone else, suffering from the effects of the Föhn, a warm wind, which followed on the snowstorm. It usually affects people badly, making them feel sticky and prickly. To make matters worse, it began a partial thaw, with the result that there was no going out until that was over. Girls and staff alike were affected. The latter seemed never to have been so hard to please, and the former, so their mistresses complained, had never been so tiresome.

In Jack's case, it increased her resentment and further sharpened her wits where mischief was concerned. She found the second packet from among her handkerchiefs late on Thursday afternoon when she was turning out her pockets in search of a missing rubber.

When she first came on it, she stared at it with wonder. She had forgotten it till then. Then her black eyes gleamed wickedly. She must use the contents. The question was—on whom? No use wasting such a thing on one of her own kind. She had already lost her cobbler's wax—and she had only one of this.

"I'm being punished, anyhow," she thought. "I shan't have a penny to spare for three weeks to come. And I've got to go and do mending on Saturday night and miss all the fun. This has been a beastly week! I'll give them something to punish me for! They can't be nastier to me than they have been!"

It might have been thought that after all the awful trouble she had been in over Margaret's tunic, she might have used a little caution. Not Jack! She went about the rest of the day with an air that mystified the rest of her own clan; but when they asked for an explanation, she refused to give one.

Len Maynard, meeting her in Hall, saw it and wondered, but as she was with two or three others, let it go, Later, she was sorry.

With the exception of the Head, Mlle and Miss Dene, the staff all slept along a side corridor on the top floor. They had their own bathrooms, opposite the entrance to the corridor. The girls were forbidden to go to the corridor or the bathrooms unless specially sent by a mistress, and how Jack found the audacity to play her trick was something no one ever discovered.

Miss Burnett, tired and sticky after a strenuous hour and a half spent on remedials, came upstairs to change for the evening, and decided to have a bath. She caught up her towels and sponge-bag, ran along to the nearest bathroom, turned on both taps and got into the bath with the idea of letting the gradual rising of the soft, velvety water soothe her.

She got more that she bargained for. The water gushed out but it wasn't water that rose up all round her, but bubbling foam! She was so startled, that she yelled aloud, even as she scrambled out again, and attracted the attention of Kathy Ferrars and Nancy Wilmot who were also changing, as well as a whole string of girls from the nearest dormitories, who all came pouring out into the corridor to demand what had happened.

Miss Wilmot banged on the door and asked what was wrong.

"Nothing!" Miss Burnett said crossly. "And go away, Nancy, do! I'll be out in a minute!" Then, in a different tone: "Oh, mercy! The taps!"

She had forgotten to turn them off and the bubbling mixture was rapidly rising over the edge of the bath. They heard her plunging across the floor and then Miss Ferrars, rousing to the fact that a pack of girls were where they had no business to be, ordered them back to their dormitories in no uncertain tones. When at last the bathroom door opened, the corridor was bare of girls and only her two colleagues were standing there, their faces alight with curiosity.

"What on earth is the matter with you?" Nancy Wilmot demanded. "Did a mouse come along, or what?"

"Don't be such an ass!" Miss Burnett was still annoyed with herself. "As if a mouse would make me yell! You go in and look at that bath! Mind where you're stepping, though," she added hastily. "The floor's a complete mess!"

The two mistresses peered into the bathroom.

"Peggy!" exclaimed Kathy Ferrars. "Have you, of all people, taken to bubble baths?"

"Of course I haven't! This is some stupid idiot's idea of a joke!"

"A joke!"

"Well, that's what it looks like. I got in and turned on both taps and it rose all round me like that. I was so stunned, I didn't even have the sense to turn the taps off until a minute or so ago. Now, I suppose, I must go and find cloths and mop it up! But this is the outside of enough! Just let me catch the perpetrator of this so-called joke, and I'll make her wish she had never been born!"

And Peggy Burnett stalked off, indignation in every movement.

"Heaven help the little ass who thought that one up!" Nancy Wilmot remarked as she turned to go and finish dressing. "Peggy's got it in for her!"

By the end of the evening, it was all over the school, of course. The girls who had heard the yell passed on the news to the rest and many were the wild guesses as to what could have happened.

Jack heard it among the rest, but kept her own counsel. She was beginning to feel rather scared now. It might have

66

been better to have used that packet of bubble bath she had taken from her mother's drawer last thing before she left home on one of their own baths.

"I did think they might come in useful for a joke," she thought, "but—"

Miss Annersley knew about it, of course. There was little that went on in the school that Miss Annersley did not know. After Abendessen, she sent for Peggy Burnett and questioned her.

"I wish you'd let me deal with it myself," Peggy pleaded when she had told the whole story. "I'm pretty sure this is a Middles' rag. In that case, I can tackle them beautifully —or her, if it's only one."

"I certainly think it wasn't a Senior—not even Prudence Dawbarn or Connie Winter," the Head said decidedly. "But, Peggy, the girls all know that they must not trespass on your quarters."

"Oh, some little idiot thought she'd be clever," Peggy said easily—she had recovered her temper by this time. "The fact of the matter is I feel rather a fool over the whole thing. If I hadn't yelled, no one would have been any the wiser. As it is, I made a fuss and now everyone knows."

The Head laughed. "It will certainly go down in our annals. I hope you're prepared for it?" she said teasingly. "Very well; I'll leave it to you. But don't let anyone off too easily, please. This sort of thing can't be allowed."

Peggy went off, pondering how she could best find out the culprit. She was saved her trouble. She went to the remedials room to seek her notebook as she wanted to write it up. She had not been there long when Len Maynard arrived, bringing Jack Lambert with her.

"Please, Miss Burnett, Jack would like to speak to you," Len said. She spoke seriously, but her eyes were dancing. As for Jack, she was staring at the floor.

She had bumped into Len, who had taken one look at her and then marched her off to a quiet corner to ask "And what's been wrong with you all day?"

By this time, Jack was regretting her prank as hard as she could go. She had heard what the rest had to say about messing about with one of the staff bathrooms and she realised that she had been abominably impertinent, to say the least of it.

She looked at Len doubtfully. "I—I expect it's the weather," she muttered.

"Weather my foot!" Len commented simply. "You've been up to some silly—Jack Lambert! Was it you who fooled about with a staff bathroom?"

"I—I—ye-es," Jack owned very sheepishly.

"You little lunatic! What was it?"

"A packet of bubble bath."

Len stared and then hastily swallowed.

"Where did you get it?" she asked when she could control her voice again.

"I—I snaffled them from a box Mother has."

Len's lips quivered. "Without telling her, of course?"

"We-ell—"

Once more, Len had a struggle to control herself. She won it and then said gravely, "But, Jack, why use it on a staff bathroom? You know that we are forbidden to go to those quarters, don't you?"

Jack nodded.

"But, my lamb, that makes it even worse. You've broken a strict rule. You've been cheeky to a mistress — for it was outrageous cheek, let me tell you!—and you did it knowing quite well that it was forbidden."

Jack was crimson. It sounded rather awful when it was put plainly before her.

"What are you going to do about it?" Len demanded suddenly.

Jack suddenly looked up. Len's lips were quite grave, but her eyes were dancing.

"I s'pose I'd better go and own up," she blurted out.

"And apologise, too. It really was disgraceful cheek! OK. Want me to come along and hold your hand, metaphorically speaking?"

68

Jack stared at her blankly. Len saw she did not understand.

"Come along," she said. "I'll take you to Miss Burnett and you can get it over. I expect she'll be pretty stiff with you, but remember that you asked for it. It was awfully silly of you. Didn't you have enough fuss over Margaret Twiss's tunic?"

Jack gulped. Then something gave way and it all came tumbling out.

"Oh, I don't know—I honestly don't! It was having the things in my pocket—and—and I was mad at Margaret and I've gone on being mad about things—and I didn't think. I just did it!"

Len nodded. "I see. Well, now you've got to put it right as far as you can. That's only the decent thing to do. Tell Miss Burnett what you've told me and say how sorry you are. She'll punish you, of course, but you expect that. But, Jack, do try to think before you play any more jokes. It's so silly to go on getting yourself into frantic rows, and not worth it, either."

She slipped a hand through Jack's arm and steered her along to the remedials room where, as she expected, Miss Burnett was busy. She pulled Jack in after her, made her announcement and then withdrew to a distant point to await the culprit when the games mistress had finished with her. She expected that Jack would be ready for a little help.

Peggy Burnett looked up in amazement at Len's words. As that young person closed the door behind her, her gaze moved to the sinner and, annoyed as she was, her lips trembled a moment. Jack looked so thoroughly hangdog.

"Well?" she said, rather more kindly than she had meant. "What is it, Jack?"

"Please," Jack said, "it was me—me that gave you a bubble bath, I mean—"

The odd way of putting it was too much. Peggy Burnett dropped her pen and burst into shrieks of laughter. Jack stared at her in amazement. However, the mistress pulled herself together.

"I see," she said. "You do know, don't you, that you aren't allowed to interfere with any of our rooms?"

"Ye-yes!" Then Jack summoned up her courage and repeated the tale she had told Len. Peggy listened to it with a twinkle in her eyes, but she said nothing until the sinner had reached the end of her story.

"I see," she said. "Have you any more bubble bath hidden away?"

"Oh, no!" Jack said fervently. "Mother would have missed them if I'd taken more than one packet."

"Ah! That's as well." Again there was silence while Miss Burnett cogitated. At last, she spoke. "Anything more to say?" she inquired amiably.

"Yes. Please, I'm sorry I did it. I didn't mean to be cheeky, only—well, I thought it was a pity to waste bubble bath on any of our crowd and—and—" Jack ran down there, not being very sure how to wind up her peculiar apology

"I see. I accept your apology, Jack, but I'm afraid you must repeat it to all the other mistresses. It might have been any of us, you see, so the sin is against all of us. You must learn that you can't do things like that. Tonight, the radio promised us a sudden drop in temperature. That means that we should be able to have skiing and coasting again by Monday at latest. I'm sorry, but you must miss the first day of it. Instead, you will go for an ordinary walk with someone. Of course, after this long period of being shut in, you must have outdoor exercise. Now you may go. After Prayers, come to the staff room and then you can apologise to everyone else. Run along and don't be so silly again."

Jack went. It was a horrid punishment, but it had to be borne somehow. And, thank goodness, only the mistresses would know about the apology!

Len was faithfully waiting for her.

"Got it over?" she said as Jack reached her.

Jack nodded. "She—she wasn't too bad, but I—I've got to miss the first day of winter sports and—and—I've got to go and apologise to all the mistresses after Prayers."

70

Len was deeply sympathetic, but all she said was, "Well, you knew you'd have to pay somehow, didn't you? As for Margaret, Jack, don't scrap with her and, above all, don't play tricks on her. It isn't kind."

Jack had nothing to say to that and Len felt she had said all she could for the moment. She sent the junior off and went to Va, hoping devoutly that with the change of weather would come a change of atmosphere.

Chapter 8

Len Butts In

EVERYTHING comes to an end at last. Jack had a bad moment when, escorted by Miss Burnett, looking very official, she walked into the staffroom. Every mistress the school possessed seemed to be there. They knew what was coming and when Peggy Burnett and her victim arrived, they all stopped what they were doing and turned severe looks on Jack, who felt scared almost out of her wits. Standing under that battery of eyes, she went first red and then white. For two pins, she would have turned tail and fled. Only the knowledge that she wouldn't be allowed to get far and a certain pride held her.

"Pup-please," she said, her voice getting squeakier and squeakier as she went on, "I'm very—sorry for—being so cheeky—and—and I'll n—never d—do such a thi—ing again."

Mlle, as the doyenne of the staff, had been appointed spokeswoman. She came across the floor to where Jack stood, winking fiercely to keep the tears back.

"But of course we forgive you," she said. "You will not forget again, will you? And now, ma petite, it is time for bed for you, n'est-ce pas? You must make haste to your dormitory. Bonne nuit! Le bon Dieu te garde!" She stooped to kiss the repentant sinner on both cheeks and thereby nearly finished Jack's self control.

Peggy guessed it and bundled her out of the room in short order. "Off you go to bed!" she said with a friendly spank. "Sleep well!"

Jack scuttled off, swallowing her sobs as she went. She was thankful that everyone else was in her cubicle when

72

she reached the dormitory, for no one saw how nearly she was overcome. She spent a moment or two fighting the tears back, and won. When the prefect on duty came to switch off the lights, she was in bed and sleeping soundly.

Next day came, clear and bitterly cold. To quote Miss Armitage, the second science mistress, the bottom had dropped out of the thermometer overnight and the ground was frozen to an iron hardness that meant outdoor fun for everyone. The day before, Gaudenz had dug paths to every outside door at the school. Jack was very downcast when the Head announced at Frühstück that as soon as all dormitory work was done, everyone was to change into skiing suits and go out for a morning of either skiing or coasting. She knew that she would go out all right, but oh! it wouldn't be to winter sports!

Len happened to meet her and she saw the dejected look on the cheeky little face. Being Len, she decided to do something about it. She sped off to the remedials room, where she found Miss Burnett in the act of pulling on the yellow cap that matched her ski suit.

"Please," she said, "may I be the one to take Jack for her walk?"

Peggy Burnett turned to stare at her. "You? I was going to ask Matron Henschell to take her when she goes to St. Nicholas to discuss something with Matron there."

"Won't that be rather hard lines on Jack?" Len said persuasively. "I mean if Bar—I mean, Matron Henschell is in that direction, she'll probably go on and Jack will have to go past the meadow and see all the others having fun when she isn't. I would take her towards Ste Cécilie."

"But what about missing your own fun?" Peggy asked, looking up at the tall girl with a query in her face. "Have you thought of that, Len?"

"Oh, I've thought about it," Len replied. "The point is that I feel that, to a certain extent, some of this is my fault."

"Your fault? How?"

"Well, I knew that Jack was all revved up and I meant

to get hold of her and find out what was wrong, only I forgot. If I had, the chances are that your bath mightn't have happened."

Miss Burnett went pink. "I hope you people mean to forget that silly incident as fast as you can."

"Oh, we couldn't!" Len said with a giggle. "It'll become one of our legends! Would you have forgotten it if it had happened when you were a kid at school?"

"No; I suppose not. But I want to know why you should give up your fun for Jack. You aren't a prefect."

"Not a school prefect; but I am young Jack's dormitory prefect and I did see that she was boiling up for something and didn't do anything about it. So I'd like to take her for her walk."

"Please yourself," Miss Burnett said, laughing. "So long as you keep her out in the open air and on the move, you're welcome to the imp!"

Len chuckled. "She's an imp, all right, but a nice imp. Anyhow, she hasn't had a chance to get me to herself this past four days or more and I'll bet she's cram full of questions she wants answered. Honestly, Miss Burnett, I never knew such a kid for wanting to know!"

"Not like her Aunt Gay, then!" Peggy retorted. "I was a prefect when Gay was in the Fifth and from all I ever heard, she was quite content to scramble through her lessons with the minimum of work."

"Jack," said Len solemnly, "is the original animated question mark! I sometimes wonder what she thinks I am. Anyhow, I'll take her out this morning and get the worst over. Thank you very much, Miss Burnett."

She left the remedials room. Peggy Burnett, looking after her, thought deeply. "Len is her own mother over again! Jo used to butt in everywhere if she thought it was needed. So, for that matter, did Mary-Lou these last years. It looks to me as if both their mantles have fallen on young Len. Unless I miss my guess, that kid is slated for Head Girl before she's through!" A bell broke in on her meditations and she had to snatch up her belongings and fly.

Meanwhile, Len, having changed into her boots and found her alpenstock, went to seek Jack. She found her waiting in the Junior Middles' Splashery, looking very downcast.

"Ready?" Len said briskly. "Come on, then! I'm taking you for a good sharp trot, so be prepared."

Jack cheered up visibly. "Can we talk English all the time?" she asked.

"Not only can, but may and must. This is Saturday — English day—or half day, anyhow. Got your alpenstock? Then pull on your mitts and put your glasses on and let's be off! How good a walker are you?"

"I once walked ten miles with Daddy," Jack said, fastening her snow-goggles and wriggling her hands into her mitts. "I'm ready now."

"Then come on! Sure you're warmly wrapped up? The air's like a knife outside!"

"I'm warm enough," Jack said, following her out into the sunlit garden. She gasped as she felt the cutting cold on her face. "Coo! Isn't it icy!"

"It is; but you'll soon get used to it. Anyhow, we aren't going to saunter, I can assure you. Turn left. I have to call at home first."

Len was carrying a big bundle in her free arm. Jack tried to take it from her when they first set out, but was told that she would have all she could do to keep her feet, even with nailed boots and her alpenstock. Now Len explained as they set off along the highroad.

"This is a knitted patchwork blanket for old Frau Hüber who lives at Ste Cécilie. She's nearly crippled with rheumatism, poor old soul, and the last time Papa was there, she complained of the cold. So the staff have been knitting this for her and Mamma has been busy with another. She lives alone, except for her goats."

"Goats? Has she goats? How many? What are they like? Has she any baby goats?"

Len laughed. "I don't know how many she may have now. I believe she got rid of last year's kids while we were away during the summer. She'll still have Hanni, her big nannygoat. Hanni'll be shut up in the shed for the winter now, but if you go to Ste Cécilie later when the snow's gone, you'll probably see her, tethered to a stake. There won't be any kids at present, though there probably will be later. Turn in here. This is our house—Freudesheim."

Jack looked with interest at the house—a big, four-storey affair, with rows of windows across the front. The door was round at the side and Len explained that there were six steps up to it, though now the surface of the snow was level with the top step. Then she opened the door into a wide hall and led the way down the hall to a door which she opened.

"Mamma!" she said. Then she beckoned Jack to come in. "She isn't here! I expect she's upstairs with the babies. You sit down and wait while I go and hunt her up. I shan't be a minute."

She left Jack to find herself a seat and scampered off upstairs. She found her mother in the playroom at the top of the house, walking up and down with a baby on either arm. As Len's bright face peered round the door, her own lit up, but she kept on walking.

"What's sent you here?" she demanded softly. "Don't yell, my love! We've had a night of it with these two. They're nearly asleep now and I'm hoping they'll go off and I can put them down for a good nap, poor lambs! What have you come for, Len?"

"To bring you this from the staff," Len explained. "I'm taking Jack Lambert for a walk. She's played everyone all ends up this week and landed herself with no fun as a result. I wanted you to come down and speak to her. She's Gay Lambert's niece. But I suppose—" She halted doubtfully.

"I certainly can't do anything until these two are safely asleep. Put that thing down somewhere and run and ask Rösli to come upstairs now. I think they'll be off shortly and I've piles to do when they are. Gay Lambert's niece, you said? Yes; I remember Auntie Hilda said something about her nieces coming this term. They'd better come along for tea—now let me see. Tomorrow week, I think. I'll give Auntie Hilda a ring some time today and fix it up properly. Are you three all right. Good! And Ruey? Scoot and call Rösli. Kiss me goodbye and fly! I'll be seeing you!"

Len kissed her, gave a fond look at each of the babies, now fast asleep in their mother's arms and then went out quietly to seek Rösli, known in the family as "the Coadjutor", and send her up to help put the babies into their cots. That done, she returned to the salon and called Jack out once more.

"I wanted Mamma to come down and meet you," she explained as they set off at a good round pace, "but the babies are teething and have had a bad night and she was just getting them off to sleep, so she couldn't come. She'll be having you and Anne to tea one Sunday shortly."

"Will she?" How frightfully decent of her! Have you always lived in Switzerland, Len? Your daddy's a doctor, isn't he? Did he start the big San?"

Len laughed. "Aren't you ever tired of asking questions? No; then we've only lived out here six years—seven years in August. Yes, Papa is a doctor and he came out here to be Head of the Sanatorium staff when it was first opened. Now you stop asking questions and see what you can do about answering some for a change."

Jack grinned. "How are you to find things out if you don't ask questions?" she demanded pertinently. "I like to know!"

"I'll say you do!" Len retorted. "You can give it a rest for a moment, though, and let me have a chance. I want to know what sent you off the handle all this week."

Jack went crimson. "I—I don't know. I think really it was finding the cobbler's wax that did it."

"Where on earth did you get hold of the stuff?" Len demanded.

"I pinched it from my brother," Jack explained.

"Does he know yet? Or haven't you told him?"

"Oh, I expect he'd find out before he went to school," Jack said airily. "He'd guess where it went all right! I expect he's cursed me pretty badly if he happened to want it."

"Jack! You really are the outside of enough!" But Len nearly had the giggles. "I should think he has cursed you, as you say. I know what my brother would do if one of the kids played him a trick like that."

"Oh, have you a brother?" Jack asked curiously.

"Five of 'em—counting Geoff. I really meant Stephen, the eldest of them."

"Is he older than you or younger?" Jack wanted to know.

"Younger—and you stop trying to sidetrack. I want to get to the bottom of all this. I told you to stop asking questions for the present," Len scolded.

"Oh, sorry!" Jack went red again. She slipped a hand through Len's arm. "I—I wasn't trying to be 'quisitive. Honestly, I wasn't."

"I know." Len spoke with great solemnity. "You only wanted to know. Well, now I've told you, so hold your horses and let me have a chance. Why did you play such a trick on Margaret Twiss? She's not a pal of yours, I know. At least, I've never seen you together. You've chummed with Wanda von Eschenau and her clan, haven't you?"

Jack nodded. "I like Wanda. She's an awfully good sort, and so are Arda and Renata. We four are pals."

"But what's wrong between you and Margaret?"

"I don't know—honestly, I don't. Margaret took a hate at me when I first came, though I can't see why. So anyhow, I thought if that was the way she felt, I'd do my share, too. And I did!" Jack giggled as she remembered Margaret's face when she found her chair coming up with her. "Oh, it was funny! I turned round to see and she looked pussystruck!"

Once more, Len had to fight against her own mirth. She overcame it and said seriously, "Yes; but you can't go round ruining other people's clothes just because you've taken a hate at them."

"O—oh! I hadn't thought of that!"

78

"There are jokes and jokes. Some are the outside of enough, and anything that deliberately damages other people's property *is* the outside of enough."

"I didn't think about its making a mess of her gymmer," Jack said. She swallowed. Then her natural honesty came to the surface. "All I wanted was for other people to laugh at her and—and to take her down a peg or two."

"But, my lamb, if that was what you wanted, why on earth didn't you use that bubble bath of yours on her and let the staff alone?" Len cried. "I don't say I think it was a good idea to try to take her down a peg or two; but at least you'd have got your laugh without tearing her tunic every which way or letting yourself in for such a row with the mistresses. Honestly, Jack, you simply must try to stop and think before you do mad things, or goodness knows where you'll land yourself! With a Head's Report, most likely, and you won't like that!"

"Well, I'm not going to rag the mistresses again, anyhow," Jack told her cheerfully. "It doesn't pay."

Once more, Len was on the verge of giggles. She bit her lips fiercely and then said with some severity, "I hope you'll stick to that. And stop hating people—or saying you do. You don't really, you know. You wouldn't want to shove Margaret over the edge, would you?"

"Of course I wouldn't! That would be murder!" Jack cried indignantly.

"Well, if you bother to remember, we're told in the Bible that whoever hates his brother—and that means his fellow creatures, in case you haven't got it—is a murderer. So now where are you?"

"Gosh!" was all Jack said. But Len had given her something to think about.

Len herself realised this. She decided that she had said all she need for the moment and changed the subject as they reached a stout wooden bridge crossing a frozen stream. The bridge ran quite a long way down the path on either side before it ever reached the stream. Jack

79

eyed it with interest and promptly demanded, "Why does it go so far on away from the water—the bridge, I mean?"

"Because," Len said, "when that stream floods, it floods! The Christmas term before last we were out for a picnic and got caught in a thunderstorm and had to shelter in a barn—round that bend in the road. When it was over we set off for home again, we found that we had to wade across a pond, not a brook. And anything like the force of the water when we reached the stream itself I never felt. It nearly took us off our feet. It was quite an adventure, I can tell you."

"Golly! Did anyone fall down? Did you have to go very deep into the water? How did the escort mistresses manage? Weren't you all awfully wet by the time you got through? Why—"

Len stood still and clapped her hands over her ears. "For pity's sake stop boiling over with questions!" she exclaimed. "I never knew such a kid as you! Now stop it and I'll tell you the whole yarn. But," she added warningly, "if you ask so much as one question while I'm doing it, I'll stop. We must turn now, or we'll be late getting back."

They went at a good pace, Len telling the story of that eventful picnic to an enthralled Jack. By the time it was finished they were back at school and no more was said about the Junior Middle's sins. But that night, when Len went up to bed, a small voice called her into the cubicle where Jack was sitting up, waiting for her.

"Len! Is that you? Can you come here for a minute?"

"Yes; but keep your voice down and don't wake the others, whatever you do. You ought to be asleep yourself, anyhow. What's wrong, Jack?"

"Nothing—only—well, I thought I'd like you to know that I'm going to tell Margaret I'm sorry I did her gymmer in tomorrow."

Len gasped as she sorted this out. Then she nodded. "Good for you! But Jack, don't be surprised if she doesn't take it awfully nicely. That was a new tunic last term and her mother may have things to say about it when she goes home."

"I don't see what she can say. It's got a whole new back in. Matey's stopped my pocket money for three weeks to pay for it—all but church collections. It's like a new one—at the back, anyhow. Only, if she does things to me, I may try to get my own back," Jack said calmly.

"If you don't do things to her, there's no reason for her to do them to you," Len told her. "You make up your mind to ignore her if she makes a pest of herself. No need for you to copy her in that, at any rate."

"I don't mean to copy her," Jack announced. "I think you'd be a lot nicer copy and that's what I'll aim at. That's all I wanted to say. Goodnight!" And, very red, she dived under the clothes, leaving an equally scarlet Len to tuck them round her and murmur good night before she took herself off to her own cubicle where she did some fairly deep thinking as she got ready for bed. "It looks as if I'll have to keep an eye on myself," was her final conclusion. "Oh, bother Jack Lambert! What did she want to say that for?"

Chapter 9

COMMENTS FROM THE STAFF

"At last! Peace, perfect peace—at least we'll hope so!" Miss Derwent dropped into a big arm-chair.

Miss Charlesworth, lounging in another, looked up and laughed. "Poor Ruth! What's been happening?"

"Oh, this and that! For one thing, I've been going through Vb's ideas of an essay on TRAVEL. Twenty-six essays are something of a chore. Just consider it. There are sixteen Continentals in that form and though one or two of them can write nearly as fluently as they speak, the bulk have only to put pen to paper to become completely stilted. As for all the clichés they use, where they get hold of them I can't imagine."

"Oh, they find them floating around in the air. Never mind; this is Friday night, when we're free from everything, and tomorrow afternoon we have only to take the little dears along to St. Luke's Hall for the pantomime. You give it a miss and let shop alone."

"Hear, hear!" Rosalind Moore, head of the geography department, cried. "Not," she added, "that I think we're likely to do that for any length of time. Would someone like to change the subject?"

Before anyone could respond to this challenge, the door opened and the Head arrived accompanied by her partner, Miss Wilson from St. Mildred's, the finishing branch.

Miss Wilson was greeted with shouts of welcome. She had been at the school a term longer than Miss Annersley, but when it had been decided to open the finishing branch in the Oberland a year before the school proper was brought out to Switzerland, she had been appointed Head of that and remained Head ever since. She had been science mistress at the school for many years and when she left to take up her new appointment, someone else had had to take her place—a Miss Armitage. Two or three years ago she had married, and a young cousin of hers had been offered the post. Since St. Mildred's was on the Platz and Davida Armitage was very young when she was appointed, she worked under "Bill", as she was known among the girls. That lady took over the senior science classes and Vida Armitage was responsible for everything under Va. So the school got their beloved Bill back in part.

Bill now strolled across the room to an inviting chair, sat down and beamed on the assembled staff. 'This is a warm welcome," she remarked. "What do you all want?"

"Nothing!" Miss Moore retorted. "Can't we show our pleasure at having you without you suspecting us of ulterior motives? What a mind you've got, Nell!"

Bill laughed as she accepted the coffee Vida Armitage brought her. "How insulting!"

"You were the insulting one first!"

"Well, you must admit that to be greeted like a long-lost relative has rather a suspicious sound. However, I'll forgive you and we'll let it go. What were you all discussing when we came along?"

"Ruth's essays from Vb," Nancy Wilmot replied. A more sluggish lot I never yet met! There are times when I yearn to set off a couple of hand grenades under them. Barring some six or eight, they seem content to sit and let you pour information into them."

"What about Prudence Dawbarn?" a voice in the background demanded.

"Prudence keeps all her brains for plotting evil doings. When it comes to hard work, she's as dumb as the rest—or seems to be."

"Well, you've got seven bright sparks," remarked someone else.

"Seven! Out of twenty-six! That's a nice proportion, isn't it?" Nancy Wilmot turned to Miss Annersley who, as usual, was sitting back and taking everything in. "Hilda! Last summer you woke that crowd up pretty vigorously. Can't you do something about it now? Otherwise, I don't mind telling you that we look like having a Va of about ten, next year. Besides, one's got to look ahead. In a few years' time that lot will be our prefects. A sweet lot of prefects they will be!"

The two Heads lookd at each other and laughed. The staff were on to them at once.

"What have you got in mind?" Ruth Derwent cried.

"Tell us what you're going to do!" Nancy pleaded. "I hope it's something really drastic because I'm convinced that nothing but really drastic measures will ever wake that lot up for keeps."

"It's drastic all right." Bill said with a chuckle. "I rather think those young women are shortly going to wish they had never been born!"

"What have you two been plotting for them?" Nancy implored the Heads. "I only hope it's something they won't forget in a hurry."

Miss Annersley laughed. "When the day before half term comes, I'm summoning them to the study and I shall tell them exactly what we all think of them. When that's over, they will be told that they have the rest of this term to show a definite improvement. After that, anyone who doesn't keep it up will be sent down to Inter V and will stay there for the whole term, only returning to Vb with the next Christmas term."

Nancy whistled under her breath. "What a swingeing punishment. Yes; I should think that would hold them all right."

"That is what it's meant to do," Hilda Annersley replied, her mouth set grimly.

Bill looked round the staff. "Can anyone say how this has happened? We always have had our fair share of lazy girls and games-mad girls, but never in such quantity before. What's been going on that a whole form, more or less, can be labelled like that?"

No one could quite say. Vb had been nuisances when they were Inter V, but it had been hoped that the Head's threat that if this sort of thing went on, they would be known as Inter IV and Senior Middles, would wake them up. It had, for the time being; but once they were Vb and quite definitely seniors, they seemed to have sunk back.

"They're such a let-down after last year's Vb," Kathy Ferrars said with a sigh. "Think what they were like! Live wires and keen as mustard on *some* lessons and working at the others, anyhow."

"Think what they had in the way of members!" Miss Charlesworth pointed out. "They all worked hard."

"But this year's lot has Pen and Margot and Ruey and Primrose, who seem to keep the first four places every fortnight. And then you get Maria and Tina and Francie. After that, you have the tail. And a very dull, unenterprising tail it is!"

Miss Wilson had been exchanging glances with her co-Head. "I think," she said, "that by the time they've had that very official summons to the study and heard all Hilda has to say to them, you'll find that they'll do something about it. I know that I'm supposed to have a rasping tongue, but, as some of you ought to know from past experience, once Hilda really begins, she can beat me any day of the week."

They all laughed and the tension slackened.

"I'm sorry for the six or eight who have really worked," Ruth Derwent said. "It doesn't seem very fair for them to come in for a blowing-up."

"Unfortunately, they can't be left out. This is a form affair, so they must share it." Bill mused silently a moment. Then she went on. "I rather think you'll find that people like Pen and Co. will make it their business to see that it doesn't happen again."

"Well, they're a dull bunch, say what you will," Vida Armitage declared. "I think the pity of it is that they're all together. If they were more scattered through the forms, it wouldn't be so noticeable and some of them might be more inclined to get down to things." Suddenly, she began to laugh. "Ah, well, at least we have a nice contrast to them in the Junior Middles! Those infants in Lower IIIa, for instance."

Bill sat up. "What's the latest?" she demanded crisply.

"Nothing out of the way," Sharlie Andrews told her. "Since Jack gave Peggy that bubble bath, they've calmed down a little."

Miss Bertram, who was form mistress to Lower IIIa, nodded. "Jack is certainly calming down a little. I rather think Len Maynard is by way of taking that crew in hand."

Miss Annersley had set down her empty cup. Now she spoke. "Joan, why do you say that Len has taken them in hand?"

"It's things I've noticed—and overheard. I was going past their form room yesterday. The door was open and they were talking at the tops of their voices as usual. I heard Wanda say, 'What do you think about it, Jack?' and Jack replied, 'We'd better ask Len first. She'll tell us if it's OK or not.' As I didn't want to eavesdrop, I looked in and suggested that they'd better stop yelling about their doings if they didn't want to be overheard." She laughed. "You could have heard a pin drop after that!"

"Len Maynard," said Nancy Wilmot with decision, "is cut off the same piece of cloth as Mary-Lou Trelawney. Oh dear, how I miss that girl! Does she keep the rest on the straight and narrow path at St. Mildred's as she did here, Nell?"

"She does—not that it ought to be so necessary. But Mary-Lou sets the pace for them. That girl's a born leader. Are you telling me that my god-daughter is running on those lines now? Well, I suppose it was to be expected. Think what her mother was like!"

"I'd forgotten Joey," Nancy admitted. "Of course she was just the same. Well, Len is certainly on those lines. She sees things that need doing and butts in and does

86

them. That was Joey all right, as I well remember from my own early days."

Rosalie Dene got up to take her cup to the tray. "So that's the latest, is it? I noticed that she was letting Con and Margot go their own way, more or less. High time, too! At their age, they ought to be standing on their own feet and not relying on someone else to pull them out of scrapes."

Kathy Ferrars nodded. "It's done Con all the good in the world. She's not nearly so moony as she used to be."

"I think," Mlle said carefully, "that Margot is herself responsible for not leaning on Len. But helping others is born in Len. She's leaving her sisters alone, but quite evidently she is taking on Jack and Co. I've no fault to find with that. They need something that she can give them and, in any case, it's a very different thing."

"Of course," Nancy Wilmot took her turn, "you can all see where this is leading. When the time comes, Len will be Head Girl. What's more, she'll be Head Girl on the same lines as her own mother and Mary-Lou. And Con will be a prefect all right. I wonder if you people have noticed how she's grown up this last term or two? This time last year she was still just a little girl in many ways. Now she is quite definitely a Senior. As for Margot, I don't know. She's been a problem, hasn't she?"

"But she has improved out of all recognition," Kathy Ferrars cried. "And she really has buckled down to work in good earnest. She's top of that form every fortnight and has been both this term and last. I've sometimes wondered about suggesting that she should be moved up."

The Head smiled. "No; I'm not going to move Margot up until the end of the year. But then, if she has continued as she's been doing this past term-and-a-half, she will go straight into VIb and miss Va. However, I don't want her to know till much nearer the time, so please don't even hint at it, any of you."

They murmured assent.

"As for Len," she continued, "she, like Mary-Lou, is a

leader. She has always led in her own form. I'm glad to know she is now coming out as a leader for the younger ones. And I'm more than glad to hear that she's keeping an eye on Jack Lambert. That young woman can bear it! She's a monkey, if ever there was one!"

Chapter 10

MARGOT ASKS FOR HELP

MARGOT Maynard sat on the ottoman under her window and stared out. It was the first full day of half term and Margot was miserable.

What a ghastly interview they had yesterday with the Head! Surely she couldn't really mean what she said! But if she did—and she was not in the habit of saying things she didn't mean—then Margot would never have the chance of being with her sisters in form again.

"And it isn't my fault!" Margot thought. "I've worked like mad myself, even though it's been the most ghastly bore sometimes. I've been top of the form every time last term and this and I don't see what more I can do! I can't make the others work if they don't want to and I should think Auntie Hilda might see that."

Voices from the garden broke the thread of this and she looked out. Down below were Len, Con and Ruey with Rosamund Lilley, Ricki Fry and Francie Wilford, their chosen guests. Len glanced up and saw the unhappy face at the window. She waved gaily and shouted something. Margot pushed the lattice open with a little shiver, for the air was bitterly cold, for all the bright sunshine.

"What did you say?" she called down.

"I said, 'Scram and get ready and come after all!'" Len shouted back. "Why don't you? It's a gorgeous day for skiing! Buck up, Margot! I'll wait for you and the rest can go on. We'll soon catch up with them!"

The front door shut with a slam that shook the house and Len came clattering up the stairs at a great rate.

From her window, Margot could see the others setting off. Then Len was at the door, pulling off her mittens.

"Come on, Margot! The others can't get awfully far ahead of us. They've got Ted with them and she'd hamper anyone trying to go fast. I'll give you a hand. Where are your boots and ski things?"

"Downstairs in the cloakroom; but I don't know that I feel like going, anyhow," Margot said slowly.

Len gave her a quick glance. The laughter left her eyes and her voice was warm with sympathy as she said gently, "Is it anything I can help in?"

Margot shook her head. "I don't see how anyone can help. But thanks a million, all the same."

"Would it be any use asking Mamma?"

"No; I said I didn't think anyone could help—not even her."

Len tucked a hand through Margot's arm and pulled her down on the bed beside her. "Tell me, Margot! Even if I can't actually help, things never seem so bad once you've talked them over with somebody. We're triplets! What hurts you hurts me. We might be able to think of something betwen us. Tell me what's wrong."

Len's voice was warm and coaxing and Margot felt it. But she was not yet ready to discuss her trouble. "I don't think I can talk about it. Not at present, anyhow. Help me to get ready and I'll come with you. Find my boots and skis and sticks for me while I change, will you?"

Len looked at her again. Margot had got off the bed and was changing at top speed. Her face was hidden, for she had turned her back on her sister. There was nothing more to be done at present but to go and hunt up her possessions. Len left the room and presently the two of them were skimming over the frozen snow together. All things considered, Len decided to leave the question of Margot's trouble alone for the moment and she chattered about the St. Mildred pantomime, which had duly come off the previous Saturday and been a tremendous success.

"Wasn't Hilary priceless as the Witch Queen?" she

asked. "And really, considering that no one could truthfully say she was a great actress, I thought Verity did awfully well. Of course, her voice is lovely."

The swift movement through the bright air was helping to dispel some of Margot's unhappiness. She sounded more like herself as she responded, "Yes; she scores there, though she'll never sing like Mother. But she wasn't at all bad as Snow White and whoever wrote the thing kept her pretty level. There was nothing dramatic about the part. Oh, Len! Didn't she look weird with black hair? I'd no idea it would make such a difference to her, had you?"

"None at all. It rather took my breath away, it altered her so. But she did look rather lovely." Len suddenly giggled. "If she ever commits a crime and has to fly she can always dye her hair black and I'm sure no one would recognise her. It would be a complete disguise!"

Len was thankful to see her sister's face without the unhappy look it had worn ever since the morning before. She continued to chatter gaily about the pantomime until they reached the advance party.

Con's face lit up at the sight of both her triplets. "Oh, you changed your mind after all, Margot? Good! We'd have got further, I may say, if Ted hadn't just thrown a most gorgeous somersault! She went clean head over heels and how she didn't snap either of her skis is a mystery!" Her face suddenly dimpled—she was the only one of the triplets to sport dimples—as she added, "The only thing better that I've seen is Emmy doing the splits— remember?"

It says much for the effect of the fresh air, sunshine and Len's jolly chatter that Margot's response to this was to shriek with laughter. It had been a very funny episode, made funnier by Emerence's face when she discovered what she had done.

"How on earth did she manage it?" Ricki asked.

"Goodness knows!" Con bubbled. "She did it! It's one of my choicest memories!"

Ted grinned. "I haven't achieved the splits, but I think I must have done about everything else. Well, are we going to the San or are we sticking here?"

"Going to the San," Len said decisively. "Come on, folks! Ted, you take my arm and—and—"

"Take mine!" at least three people exclaimed together, all hurrying to offer an arm and nearly overturning the unsteady Ted in their eagerness.

"Woa!" she exclaimed. "If I *must* have two arms, I'll take Margot's. I don't see why, though. What's it in aid of, Len?"

"If we have time, I want a word with Soeur Marie-Anne," Len explained. "I haven't seen her all this term so far."

"Oh, so do I!" Ted agreed. taking the arms offered and bringing her feet together. "She was awfully decent to me when we were stuck all those weeks in Isolation because of the smallpox scare."

"How was she good to you?" Ricki demanded as they made a long line across the way.

"When Ted and I were bored to death she offered to give us lessons for something to do. And when she found out that Ted knew nothing of German, she insisted that we should talk it nearly all the time and even changed our lay-sister and sent us a German who didn't know a word of anything else. That's how Ted had learned so much by the time they sent us back to school," Len added. "How you loathed me for insisting on it, Ted!"

"Only at first. You see, I had visions of having to stay mute the whole time we were stuck there—especially when Ros was better and joined us and backed you all ends up! Then I caught on to the idea and just dug in at it. It paid, all right!"

Rosamund from the far end of the line, laughed. "Of course it did. And if you cursed us at first, you ended by blessing us. Always listen to your Auntie Len and Auntie Ros if you want to do well—ow!"

Con gave her a shove and she nearly went over. She

recovered her balance by a miracle, and rejoined the flying line, laughing.

Margot chuckled. "You know, Ted, you were an awful shock to us when you came back from San talking German quite as well as most folk, after insisting that you didn't know a word of it when you first came."

"It was quite true," Ted assured her. "I didn't. I got a bit of a shock myself."

By this time, they had crossed the mountain railway and were skimming along the road, beyond which the great Sanatorium, of which Dr. Maynard was head, stood above the steep track which had once been the only way down to the plain. Arrived there, they were interviewed by Matron and found that there was to be no visiting Naomi as they had hoped.

"I'm very sorry, girls, but I'm afraid it's out of the question," she said.

"Naomi isn't badly ill again, is she?" Len asked anxiously. The term before, Naomi had had a sudden relapse and for a full week had been in danger.

Matron shook her head. "Far from it. She's much better at the moment than she has been since the accident. And so, partly for that reason, partly because Dr. Morse, the big surgeon from Canada, has had a summons home which he must answer almost at once, the big operation is to take place this afternoon. The nurses are busy preparing her now."

"And will she really be all right, once she's over this?" Rosamund Lilley asked.

"We all hope so. It isn't likely that she will ever be strong enough to go in for mountaineering, for instance, but she will be practically straight again, and able to live a normal life—even, perhaps, play games, so long as she doesn't overdo it; though," Matron added, "that's a long way ahead yet."

"But it will really happen?" Rosamund insisted.

"If she comes through this safely—yes. Give me the books and the fruit and when I go to see her presently, I'll give them to her and tell her you came to see her. Any special messages?"

"Yes; tell her we're all dying to see her and hope it won't be long before she turns up at school all well and all that sort of thing," Margot said.

"Tell her that even if she doesn't come back to us but goes straight to the Millies, we still expect to see her," Len added.

"Give her our love and best wishes for a complete cure," Rosamund finished.

Matron had smiled over the messages. Now she looked at them gravely. "I will tell her all that. But girls, though everyone here will do the best possible for her, please, all of you, pray for her and for everyone concerned in the operation that it may be a success. This is the big operation, you know."

"I thought the first one was," Ricki Fry said.

"Everyone hoped it would be, but when it came to the point, her heart wouldn't stand it and they had to leave things undone which must be done now. Yes; I know you people knew nothing about it before, but that's how it was. Now they must be done, or it will be too late."

"Do you mean that if they aren't done now Naomi will die?" Ted demanded.

"No; only that she would never be really straight or able to move without a stick. If they can do what has to be done, she will throw her stick aside and be straight again."

"When is it scheduled for?" Margot asked quietly.

"Two o'clock—and it will be a long one. Now I must go. What's that, Len? Soeur Marie-Anne? I'm afraid you can't see her just now. We have seven measles cases in isolation. I can just hear Miss Annersley on the subject if I let you go there! Goodbye, girls," as a junior nurse appeared in the corridor. "I'm evidently wanted."

There was nothing for it but to say goodbye and set off home again.

Rosamund took charge. "Ted, Ricki and I will take you on now. Len and Margot did it coming, so we'll have you going. This afternoon we might come out for a while and give you some steady practice. Just at present, considering the time, we'd better get back."

They broke up into groups. Rosamund and Ricki took Ted and Con went flying ahead with Ruey and Francie, thus leaving Len and Margot who dropped behind a little.

"You know," the former said as she and her sister got into their swing, "it looks to me as if Naomi wouldn't be back at school at all. If it's going to take all that time for her to get really well, she'll be on the late side, even for Millie's."

"Still, if it means that she won't be a cripple any longer, I don't suppose that will worry her," Margot rejoined. What a girl Len was for sympathising! And how she seemed to understand other folk. "Just like Mother does," Margot thought. "What if I do tell her what's wrong? She always used to be ready to haul me out of trouble, only—well—last year—" She stopped thinking. Last year and its events still made her feel as if she would never in this world get over being ashamed of herself for what had happened.

As if she could read her triplet's mind, Len touched her arm. "Margot! Let's go round by the back of the Platz. Mamma won't mind. The rest can tell her we're coming later. It's ages since we went round that way."

Margot made up her mind. "OK. But we'll have to give the others a yell."

"Can do!" Len promptly yodelled at length, and Con and her partners heard, swung round, and came to join them.

"Anything wrong?" Con asked, her dark eyes going from one sister to the other.

"No, idiot! But we want to go round by the back. Tell Mamma we'll be a little late, will you? Oh, and you might see that there's some elevenses left for us. Don't you crowd grab the lot!"

"Sorry to see that you judge other folk by yourselves," Con said sweetly. Then she was off at full speed to escape vengeance.

"It'll be OK," Ruey said as well as she could for laughing.

"We'll tell Mrs Maynard. Come on, Francie! Con's leaving us miles behind."

They swept round and were off and Len and Margot were left alone.

"Come on!" Len said with a shiver. "The sun's shining all right, but the air's like a knife!"

Side by side, they swung away towards the mountain wall which was known to the Platz dwellers as "the back".

Margot was silent at first, but when they reached the pines that climbed up the mountain slopes she slackened pace, saying, "If we go through the trees a little way we'll be out of the wind and—and I do want help. You will tell me what you think, won't you, Len?"

Len slowed down and waited for her sister to come up with her. "Of course I will. I said so. I can't butt in on you if you don't want me; but if you do, I'm here. After all, Margot, you, Con and I are triplets. It means more!"

"Yes; it makes a difference, doesn't it? I—I mayn't always seem to remember it," Margot added shamefacedly, "but it really is there at the back of everything."

"I suppose it always will be," Len said thoughtfully. "I think it's something we couldn't get away from, however much we tried. But let that go now. What's wrong? You tell me and I'll go all out to help you."

"Oh, it's the most ghastly thing!" Margot said. "Yesterday morning, instead of coming to us for lit. as she always does after Break, Auntie Rosalie came and said the Head wanted to see us in the study!"

Len's eyebrows rose and she whistled. "My only aunt! Why on earth?"

"She said she'd sent for us to try to make us realise that as a form we were a disgrace to the school. Our standard was lower than anyone else's, even the junior forms. Next school year, we ought to be doing GCE work with the exam in view for the end of the year but, as things were, she didn't see how there would be more than three or four to enter. In that case, she was afraid we wouldn't be allowed to have our own centre as usual—"

"Oh, no!" Len interrupted, all agog with horror. "She can't have meant that!"

"Have you ever known her when she said a thing of that kind and not meant it?"

Len was silenced. Miss Annersley was noted for meaning exactly what she said in such matters.

"What is she going to do about it?" she asked anxiously.

"Oh, Len! That's the awful thing! She said we have till the end of this term to prove that we could do better. If we don't, then we're to join Inter V for the whole of next term and not go back to Vb until September."

Len looked very serious. "What is wrong with your lot, anyhow?"

"Oh, I don't know! Some of them go all out for games and can't be bothered with anything else any more than they must. And some just don't care, anyhow."

"Yes; but not all of you," Len objected. "I know that you and Ruey, at any rate, have worked like Trojans this term and last. And there's Francie Wilford and Pen Grant and one or two more who all get a fortnightly average of over 70 per cent. She can't have meant everyone!"

"She said the whole form," Margot returned miserably.

"It doesn't sound like her to me. She's always so awfully fair. She must know that you and Ruey, at any rate, have slogged the whole of last term and this. Why, you had 93 per cent last fortnight and your half-term average was 88 per cent! And Ruey was only two behind you. Even Francie was 70 per cent, for she told me so."

"But, Len, what can I do to make the others work? I can't make the idiots slog if they don't want to. And they don't!"

"I don't believe there's the slightest risk where you're concerned. But I do think the rest will have to haul up their socks and hoe in!"

Margot looked at her, hope dawning in her face. "Oh, Len, is that what you really think?"

"Shouldn't say it if I didn't. You cheer up and enjoy the rest of half term, and when we go back, go on slogging."

Margot flushed. "OK. I will! Oh, Len, what a poppet you are! I feel heaps better now. Thanks a lot!"

"Well, you're my triplet," Len said simply. She changed the subject. "Now come on, or those greedy creatures will have hogged everything. Ready? Off!"

Chapter 11

LEN STAYS AT HOME

THE rest of the half term went with a bang. Margot, relieved of her worst fears, became her usual gay self, much to the relief of Joey Maynard, who had been anxious about her.

"What's made the difference?" Jack Maynard asked that night. "Has she been chatting with you?"

Joey shook her head so violently that one of her long black pigtails swung out and hit him in the face. "Not she! She doesn't confide very much in me these days. I only wish she would. Len and Con still have seasons of babbling out everything to Mamma, but not Margot. I think it's partly because of late years she's been up against authority in every shape and form."

"That, if the pundits are to be believed, is the normal teenage attitude."

"Rot! I never felt it—and when you remember that home authority in my case meant Madge, a mere sister, it's a marvel, if they're right. Anyhow, I'm not going to try to force Margot's confidence. It must come freely or not at all. I never have believed in trying to pry into the depths of a child's soul. I'm not going to start now. If Margot has anything she wants to tell me, she knows I'm always ready to hear."

Jack came to sit down beside her. "What a good choice I made for my brats' mother! Well, it's getting late and I'm about all in. I vote for bed. Think those imps in there," he jerked his head towards the door communicating with the night nursery, "will let us have peace?"

"Oh, I expect so. The rest are all sleeping sweetly.

Unless we're visited by highly optimistic burglars, I don't think we're likely to be disturbed. Come on, and make the most of it while you have it!" Joey yawned widely. "I'm three parts asleep myself. I'll be talking in my sleep if I don't get in pronto."

He took her advice. Everyone slept peacefully until six o'clock when the telephone roused Jack. That woke Joey too, and she went promptly to see to her babies who were making little murmurs as a hint that it was time for fresh bottles. She had everything ready and was busy with little Geoff when Jack looked in, fully dressed.

"I'm off to the San," he said in an undertone. "Sister rang up to say that Naomi is in pain, so I'm going to see what I can do about it."

"Is it bad?" Joey asked fearfully.

"Can't say exactly until I've seen her. Pain is to be expected, but she is still so weak, we want to spare her all we can. I expect I can do something about it. Sister says her pulse is better and her temp's pretty fair, too. That's all I know. Now I'm off!"

He took himself off and Joey finished feeding Geoff before laying him down, already half-asleep, and attended to his twin.

This was a shorter half term than usual—from Thursday afternoon till Tuesday afternoon. The term was little more than eleven weeks long and only those girls who lived near at hand and such friends as they invited had left the school. The rest were staying and enjoying various expeditions.

"Are we going anywhere?" Margot asked at breakfast that morning.

Joey shook her head. "Not so far as I know. You'll have to wait till Papa gets back from the San to know that."

"What did he say about Naomi?" Con asked anxiously.

"She's making headway, though it's terribly slow, of course. Papa went early because she was having pain. That's only to be expected, I know, but he thought he could do something to relieve it." Joey peered out of the nearby window. "I don't believe you'll get much in the way of skiing or coasting today. It looks to me as if a thaw had started."

"Oh, Aunt Joey, no!" Ruey cried. "Why do you say that?"

"Well, see for yourself. There isn't a sparkle in the snow though the sun is shining, and it's lost that crisp look. It wouldn't surprise me if it thawed in good earnest now. What would you folk like to do with yourselves?"

"Could we go down to Interlaken this morning?" Ruey asked.

"If Uncle Jack hasn't planned something, I don't see why not. You'll have to promise to leave the lakes alone —no skating when we aren't there! Promise, please, all of you!"

"Of course we won't," Rosamund said readily.

"That's understood, then. Of course, there may be a plan. I just don't know.—More coffee, Rosamund? Pass Rosamund's cup, Felicity. Anyone else? I think I can squeeze out enough for two more cups if you don't mind filling up with milk."

They finished the coffee among them and began to clear the table. Joey went upstairs to see to the babies and everyone was well and truly occupied when the telephone rang. Len, still busy in the dining-room, shot across the hall to take the call in her mother's study.

"Hello!" she said in German. "This is Freudesheim— Dr. Maynard."

"That's clever of it," replied her father's voice. "That you, Len? I'm going to tell Auntie Hilda it's high time she taught you girls to talk sense!"

"Oh, well, you know what I meant," Len giggled. The giggles ceased. "How's Naomi this morning? Mamma said they rang for you."

"Only because she was having pain and we don't want any more of that than can be helped. She's easier now and she's certainly stronger today. So, as Uncle Philip will be on hand and it is supposed to be a free day for me, what about a trip to Montreux when I get back?"

101

"What—all of us? How do you propose to cram us all into the car. And what about your brekker?"

"I'm having it here. It won't be all. Mamma won't come. Nor the small fry. It'll mean you three, Ruey, and the visitors. Ruey has never seen Montreux, and neither, I fancy, has Ted."

"But even if it's just us, it'll mean seven and that's more than a bit of a crush. We'll be packed like sardines!"

"I'm to have the honour of breakfasting with Matron, so I must go. I'm coming straight home after that, so be ready for me! I want to get off as soon as I can, once I reach home. Hanging about generally means someone rings for me and I'm having today off! Plenty of other folk to see to anyone who needs a doctor."

"Yes; but they all think there's no one like you," Len replied.

She heard his deep chuckle. Then he hung up and she went racing upstairs where everyone else had adjourned to see to the beds.

"Margot—Con—Ruey—everyone! Buckle your stumps! Papa's coming presently and he's taking everyone to Montreux. Don't forget your money and cameras."

"Montreux! Oh, good!" Con exclaimed. "Are we going to see Aunt Winifred?"

"He didn't say. Only that everyone was to be ready to go the minute he arrived. Oh, and Naomi is definitely stronger and he was able to relieve the pain. Now I must scram and tell Mamma!"

Len dashed off up the remaining flights of stairs and reached the playroom where Joey was busy establishing the baby twins in their playpen. Small Felicity and smaller Cecil were already with the dolls and Felix was having a high old time in every sense of the word on the aged rocking-horse.

"You'll be thrown through the window if you rock like that," his eldest sister warned him. "Mamma—"

"Who was that on the phone?" Joey asked, looking up from her babies.

"Papa!" And Len poured out all the news in one burst.

"Oh, good! Montreux is a jolly good choice—not too far and yet far enough to be a real change. With luck, it should be lovely and warm, too."

"If it isn't raining when they get there," Len said cautiously.

"'They'? Don't you mean 'we'?"

"No; I'm not going."

Joey sprang to her feet and looked her first-born sternly in the eyes. "Mary Helena Maynard! If your idea is to stay at home to help me with the babies, you can think again!"

"Oh, it isn't—or only partly!" Len cried in a hurry. "I want a chat with Auntie Hilda and you know what it's like in term time. I know she's not going to be out today, so I thought I'd ring and ask if I might hop over this morning. Then, this afternoon, I want to ask Mary-Lou to have English tea with us. They don't have their half term till next weekend, you know. That OK?"

"It's quite OK by me, if that's the case," quoth Joey, who not infrequently lapsed into slang as freely as her family. "You'll have to settle with your father, though."

"I'll do that all right," Len said serenely. She threw her arms round her mother. "You're a complete poppet! I won't tell you why I want to see Auntie Hilda, if you don't mind. It isn't my secret; but I think I ought to see her."

"When have I ever tried to prise things out of you? I'm always glad to hear confidences from you girls, as you know; if you want my help, it's yours for the asking. But you need never fear that I'll try to dig anything out of you. I know I can trust you."

Len returned her look gravely. "That's a compliment," she said slowly. "Thank you, Mamma. I really will try to deserve it. Now I must fly. I'll come back when the crowd have gone off and we'll have elevenses together and I'll have you all to myself for once in a way."

Joey laughed. "As though you couldn't have that any

103

night you like! I don't come round regularly to you people now because I've felt lately that you're outgrowing it. If you want me, you've only to say so."

"I know. And, of course, we three are going on for sixteen now. It's time we stood on our own feet."

"Oh, mercy!" Joey's voice was full of horror. "Sixteen! I must be growing an elderly party when my first babies are 'going on for sixteen!' See any white hairs?"

Len chuckled. "Nary one, so don't worry. As for growing elderly, it isn't in you! We're jolly lucky to have such a young mother and we all know it! Be seeing you!" And she left the room and went clattering off downstairs to do what she could to help the expedition to get ready.

"But why aren't you coming?" Rosamund demanded when she first heard that Len was staying behind.

"I have a job on hand that I want to clear up as soon as I can. And I propose to invite Mary-Lou to tea. I miss her awfully at school, even though this is the second term since she left. If you don't mind, Ros, I'd honestly rather stay this time."

Rosamund eyed her thoughtfully. "I see. We'd rather have you with us, but if that's how you feel—OK."

"You're sure you don't mind? After all, you are my special guest," Len said earnestly.

Rosamund laughed. "No; I understand."

She turned from the mirror where she had been arranging her beret at the most becoming angle. "What shall I bring you from Montreux?"

"A bar of chocolate," Len said instantly. "You can't get much up here and I'd love some chocolate." Her quick ear was caught by the sound of the car and she tore out of the room, calling back over her shoulder, "I have to see Papa."

Downstairs, Jack Maynard was greeted by Len, who asked him with a gulp, if she might miss the trip to Montreux. "Come into the study," he said, tossing his hat down on the big chest at one side of the hall.

When they were there, he swung her round to face him. "Now then, what are you up to?"

"Nothing's wrong, honestly. There's some school business I want to talk over with Auntie Hilda and you never can get a sniff at her usually."

"And what does your mother say about it?"

"Says it's OK by her," Len replied with a deliberate quotation.

He chuckled. "She would! Very well, then. You may do as you choose. What shall I bring you back from Montreux?"

"Ros asked me that and I said a bar of chocolate."

"In that case, I'll use my own judgment. Now where are the others? I want to get off. This is supposed to be a free day for me, but if we linger here, someone's safe to ring up for me. I must see your mother. You collect the rest and get them into the car, will you?"

He was not more than ten minutes away, by which time the girls had crammed themselves into the car, all armed with their bags, cameras and raincoats. Jack came down the stairs, two at a time, caught up his hat and took his seat at the wheel. He had not stopped the engine but left her ticking over. How rightly he had judged was proved by the fact that as they started, he could hear the telephone bell ringing. But for once, he paid no heed to it. This was a free day for him and he meant to have it somehow. There were plenty of other doctors on the Platz and at the Sanatorium if the case were urgent.

Len giggled to herself as she went to take the call and it gave her real satisfaction to be able to state that Dr. Maynard was not at home and would not be until the evening, for the caller was an elderly lady who was too fond of sending for him on the slightest provocation.

Len then used the telephone on her own account, and she finally carried the tray containing the cups of steaming chocolate and the plate of tiny cakes Anna had given her up to the playroom with such a broad grin on her face that Joey, seeing it as she came into the room, instantly demanded to know the reason for it.

"And who was that on the phone?" she added as she set aside her sewing.

"Only old Miss Gray from the Rösleinalpe. She wanted Papa and was she mad when I told her he was away for the day!" Len laughed gaily. "I offered to get hold of Uncle Eugen or Dr. Morrison, but she decided to wait till tomorrow."

Joey joined in her laughter. "Oh, well, no one need feel guilty if it's Miss Gray. She sends for Papa if her little finger aches! Have you made your own arrangements all right? I heard you at the phone after Miss Gray rang off."

"Oh, yes! Auntie Hilda is walking to the San to ask how Naomi is at twelve o'clock and she asked me to go with her. I'll take Bruno and give him a run!"

"Yes, do. What about Mary-Lou? Is she coming?"

The laughter died out of Len's face. "Yes. She said I'd saved her ringing you up. She's coming about 15.30 hours. But, Mamma; I think something is wrong from the way she spoke."

"How do you mean? What did she say?" Joey asked sharply.

"It wasn't what she said. She didn't say anything more than I told you. But her voice had a queer sound. I hope there's nothing wrong with Auntie Doris."

Joey took up her cup. "So do I. Well, we can do nothing about it until she arrives. If it's private, Len, you might leave us alone, dear. And I think it may be best if I see her first. Can your business wait?"

Len nodded vigorously. "Of course it can. Anyhow, I expect Auntie Hilda will have settled things before that. It's really more her affair than anyone else's. I only wanted Mary-Lou for a standby and if she's in trouble or anything, mine can wait."

Chapter 12

EMULATING MARY-LOU

"I'M going now, Mamma. Rösli's come upstairs to the playroom. Anna doesn't need her any longer, so she can take the babies over. It's five to twelve, so I'd better get off. Can't keep Auntie Hilda waiting! She might have things to say."

Joey half-turned in her chair to survey her daughter's bright face. "Good! Thanks to you, I've had a good hour and if Rösli is upstairs, I can go on for nearly another. If you're meeting Auntie Hilda at twelve, you'd better scram."

"I'm going. What time is lunch?"

The school used the Swiss names for meals, so Joey stuck to the English ones.

"Oh, the usual time. I'll wait for you. Bring Auntie Hilda back with you. No need for her to feed alone when we're here."

"I'll ask her, but she said something about lunching at St. Mildred's with Auntie Nell."

"Well, ask her, at any rate." Joey turned back to her typing and Len slipped out to bring the family pet, a magnificent St. Bernard.

"If Mamma only knew!" she thought as she clipped his chain to his harness. "I'm not exactly looking forward to this. But I must do something when Margot's asked me. Besides, she'll go miserable again and it really isn't fair when she's slogged all this time as she has done."

She stood up and Bruno nearly knocked her flat by bouncing at her before turning to the front door with insistent whimpers.

"It's all right, old man," she said soothingly as she picked up her alpenstock with her free hand. "We really are going walkies." Then they were outside and Len was thankful that she was wearing her stout, nailed boots. The thaw had set in—not a doubt of it! The surface of the snow was slushy, even though she knew it would still be like iron below that.

She was given no chance to loiter. Bruno was wild to be off and he towed her along at a speed that got her to the school gates already breathless.

The Head was waiting for her and she laughed.

"Let him go, Len. He needs a good gallop to take the edge off his spirits." She stooped and unclipped the chain. "There you are, old boy! Scamper!"

Bruno needed no second telling. He was flying ahead in a moment, galloping round in wild circles. He barked loudly and joyously as the softening snow flew before him. They let him have his head for a minute or two. Then Len called him to heel and they set off for the tramp to the Sanatorium.

"We're going to have a thaw," Miss Annersley remarked, stopping for a moment to stamp her boots free of the clotted snow on them.

"We may quite likely get more snow and frost later on. It's early for the real thaw, Auntie Hilda," Len remarked. She was trying to brace herself to perform what she mentally called "a Mary-Lou act", and it wasn't easy.

Mary-Lou Trelawney had been noted for one thing throughout her school career. That was tackling everyone, contemporaries and elders alike, as if they were all her contemporaries. Brought up in her early years by her mother and grandmother, with practically no friends of her own age, she had arrived at the Chalet School at the age of ten with an oddly grown-up outlook on many things. What she thought, that she said without fear or favour. It was fortunate for her that most people recognised it for what it was. The result had been that over and over again she had, as her friends said, got away with things they themselves would never have dreamed of saying or doing.

Len, the eldest by half-an-hour of a long family, had been kept a little girl. Joey objected to sophisticated youngsters and had rather tended to treat them still as children when, as in the case of Margot in particular, they were beginning to feel themselves quite old enough to strike out for themselves. Len was going to try to copy Mary-Lou and it took some doing. So at first, she followed the Head's lead and chatted about surface things. But by the time they had reached the railway and got themselves and Bruno safely across, she had succeeded in screwing herself up to it and made her effort after she had let the dog run free again.

"Auntie Hilda," she began, "please, I don't want you to think me cheeky or anything like that. I honestly don't mean it that way. But—but I want to say something to you."

The Head turned a startled look on her. "My dear girl, when have I ever accused you of being cheeky? I can't imagine it happening. Say what you like. You need never think I'll misunderstand."

"You awfully easily might," Len said. "Anyhow, you will take this as off the record, won't you, and say nothing about it to her? Or not that it's me, I mean."

"Len, what *is* the matter with you? Who am I to say nothing to? Tell me what you like as you like; and certainly, I'll treat it as off the record. Now go ahead and do try to be coherent! At the moment, you've got me all muddled up!"

"It's Margot," Len blurted out. Then, having taken her first hurdle, she went at it headlong. "Oh, Auntie Hilda, she's been most desperately miserable ever since the hol began. She thinks you meant what you said about turning them all into Inter V next term to apply to everyone! You don't, do you? Margot says you told them they were lazy and careless as a form. But that doesn't apply to her—and some others, too. Only it's Margot that's on my mind just now. Honestly, Auntie Hilda, she's slogged like mad both last term and this. She's gone at it steadily—no flash-in-the-pan business this time! She's been top of the form every time and she was top of the exams last term as well. And look at her averages—never less than ninety!"

Miss Annersley listened in silence as Len went on. When at last that young lady had talked herself out, she still said nothing at first. Len, feeling rather alarmed at this continued taciturnity, stole a glance at her. Was Auntie Hilda mad with her? Before she could decide one way or the other, Bruno, who had been ranging ahead, came galloping back, flung himself on his young mistress with great enthusiasm and sent her flying into a snowdrift.

Len shrieked as he came to dig frantically at her with great paws. Miss Annersley suddenly relaxed and broke into a ringing peal of laughter as she hastened to the rescue. Len had not gone far in and she was soon up and shaking the melting snow off her coat. Bruno was no help as he tried to lick her with a loving but wet tongue and Len scolded him vigorously.

"Get down! Down, Bruno, you wretch! Sit! Sit, I say! You bad dog! Just look at my coat! I've a good mind to put you on the chain for the rest of the walk. You're a naughty, bad dog!"

Poor Bruno's tail disappeared between his legs and he looked utterly crestfallen. Len finished clearing herself of snow and then looked at him and her soft heart betrayed her. "Yes; it's all very well to look miserable about it, but you deserved every word I said. Now behave yourself for the rest of the walk like a Christian dog or you will go on the chain!" She suddenly stooped to give him a mighty hug. "All right; we're friends again. Now go to heel and don't do mad things any more."

Bruno bounced up again, grinning widely, his great tail swinging delightedly. But he kept at heel for the next ten minutes and Len went on with her story rather more calmly.

"You see, Auntie Hilda, what I'm so afraid of is that

Margot may feel that it's no use going on trying if it's going to get her nowhere."

"I see." It was the Head's first comment. Then she went on, "I'm very sorry about Margot and the other five or six who really have worked. But it won't do for just a few in the form to slog, as you say, while the rest sit back and take things as easily as then can—or dare. They needed a good shaking up and I'm hoping this may have done it."

"Oh, I see that," Len replied. "The only thing is, as Margot herself says, she may work, but she can't force anyone else."

"I think she can, to a certain degree."

Len stared at her. "But how? She can't say, 'Get on with your work!' or things like that. They just wouldn't listen to her and it would only set their backs up."

"I'm sure it would," her brevet-aunt agreed. "But there are other ways. Your own form has always had a reputation for good, steady work, even with certain people who are not naturally workers in it. Now how has that happened?"

"Why—I never thought of it before," Len said. "No one would be very loving to a slacker if she went on for long. The rest of us would soon see that she didn't go on letting the form down like that, I can tell you!"

"Exactly! In other words, it's the fashion to work in Va. That is what Margot has to do—to make solid work fashionable with her crowd. She can do it, you know. Margot is very popular, Len, and she's a leader."

Len thought it over. "I see," she said at last. "Only I don't know how she could manage it. She couldn't preach to them, you know. It wouldn't be Margot if she did and they'd soon see that and then—finish!"

Miss Annersley stopped and turned to look into the troubled eyes that always made her think of English wood violets. "Len, stop worrying! I thought you'd decided not to interfere with your sisters but let them stand on their own feet?"

"This isn't interfering, Auntie. Margot herself asked me

to help. It seemed to me that if you'd listen to what I had to say you might, perhaps, get those six or seven alone and well, tell them that what you said doesn't really apply to them." Len finished on a doubtful note.

"If they work steadily till the end of the term and really try to pull up, it won't happen at all," Miss Annersley replied. "All those who don't work will find that it does happen. Margot can't have listened to me properly. There was no need for her to be miserable, as you say, if she had paid proper attention to everything I said."

"I expect," said Len with sudden inspiration, "that Margot was so stunned by the first part she thought of nothing else."

Miss Annersley laughed. "Now," she said briskly, "you may use my hint that Margot and those other people have to do what they can to make work fashionable in their form. Don't let them think it comes from me. After that, it's up to them."

"I see." Len's face cleared. "Thanks a lot, Auntie Hilda. And thank you for understanding that I wasn't trying to be cheeky or—interfering. As a matter of fact, I was trying to do a Mary-Lou act."

"Auntie Hilda" looked at her speechlessly for a minute. Then suddenly broke into a peal of laughter. It was cut short by a shriek from Len, who had seen Bruno dive down the steep rocky pathway at the far end of the Platz, and also by wild howls from that gentleman himself. Len tore off to see what was happening, followed by a cry of, "Use your alpenstock, Len! Use your alpenstock!" from her Head Mistress, who followed her in short order.

They reached the top of the path and saw that Bruno had broken off a huge chunk of semi-frozen snow which was sliding down the pathway, while he scrabbled wildly as it carried him with it. Len dived down after him, but kept her head and used her alpenstock. The Head followed her.

Mercifully, the path zigzagged considerably and Bruno came up against a snag which checked his headlong course just long enough for the two to reach him. Plunging the iron-pointed ends of their alpenstocks into the hard snow beneath while they clutched his harness, they saved him from crashing into the rockwall where the snow which had broken from beneath him dashed itself to pieces. They had to get back to the top, but they did it after a mighty struggle, and eventually all three, badly shaken and boiling hot with the efforts they had made, stood once more on the highroad, well away from danger.

"It—it wasn't a bad imitation of an avalanche, was it?" Len said shakily as she fastened Bruno's chain. "Oh, gosh! But I do feel wobbly!"

"I don't feel any too steady myself," Miss Annersley acknowledged. "As for Bruno, he's trembling, poor beastie!" She patted his head. "Poor old boy! It was a nasty moment or two, wasn't it? Come along and we'll beg coffee from Matron. That will steady us up. And a nice drink of water for Bruno."

"Why can't he have coffee like us?" Len demanded. "He adores it."

"Does he really? Oh, well, when I was small I had a kitten that adored cocoa. We'll see what Matron has to say. Now come along."

Chapter 13

MARY-LOU BRINGS NEWS

"AUNTIE Joey! Is that you? I want to see you pronto. Can I come now?"

Joey, at the telephone, grinned to herself. "You certainly can unless something has happened to cripple you. Also, you may! Mary-Lou, I'm ashamed of you! Why do you want to come now, anyhow? I thought you were coming to tea this afternoon?"

"Oh, I am; but I want to see you alone—privately. I saw Len and the Abbess from the window, going past with Bruno about five minutes ago, so I knew the coast would be clear for at least an hour. I tore off to Bill and asked leave to come—she said it was OK. Is it OK by you? Expect me in about ten minutes." Mary-Lou slammed down the receiver, and was off to change into boots and pull on beret and coat. She made no delay, and she reached Freudesheim in little more than the ten minutes she had mentioned.

Joey had gone to the kitchen in search of coffee and biscuits and as she came into the hall, pulling a light tea-trolley after her, she heard the eager steps mounting the flight up to the house. She gave the trolley a push in the direction of the salon and ran to open the front door.

"Come in—come in! I've just got coffee ready, so we'll have a session in the salon over it. Shove your things down on the chest!" she cried.

Mary-Lou tossed down coat and beret and then sat in the nearest chair and began to unfasten her boots. "D'you mind if I just sit in my stockings?"

"Certainly I do. Do you want to catch your death of

114

cold? I'll go and fetch you a pair of slippers in half a jiffy!" And she was bounding off upstairs, more like one of her teenage daughters than a married woman with a family of eleven to her credit, to return in two minutes with a pair of moccasins which she tossed to Mary-Lou. "There you are! You take a size larger than I do, but these ought to do you all right."

Mary-Lou pulled them on. "Quite OK and jolly comfy. I'll take the trolley, shall I?"

"No, go and sit down and wait till I've poured the coffee. Then you shall tell me all about it."

Mary-Lou collapsed into a chair and sat silent. Joey eyed her askance, but made no remark. She poured out the coffee and handed a cup to the girl. Mary-Lou took it gratefully, but she shook her head at the biscuits. "I couldn't, thanks. I'm too worried to eat at the moment."

"Anna will be horribly annoyed and disappointed," Joey said. "These are her very best lemon biscuits. You simply must have two at least, for it's not so long since I had chocolate and buns with Len. I can always manage an odd cup of coffee, but I can't eat a thing at the moment. Go on, Mary-Lou!"

Mary-Lou sighed. "How peremptory! Oh, very well! But you are a bosser!"

"It strikes me you need someone to boss you. What's wrong, Mary-Lou? You look like something the cat's brought in!" Her voice suddenly changed. "There's nothing wrong at home, is there?"

"No, no! Nothing like that! I had a letter from Mother yesterday and she said she was splendid. She's got through the winter without a single cold. As for Dad, well, it's going to mean amputation, they're afraid. At the same time, he's much better than he's been for a while, so—"

"They'd better come out here afterwards as soon as he's fit to be moved. I'll write to Doris and tell her. But if it isn't them, what is it?"

Joey spoke with some anxiety. Mary-Lou usually had a

fresh complexion, but today she was pale and her very blue eyes were without their usual sparkle.

"It's—look here, Aunt Joey, how much do Ruey and the boys care about their dad?"

"Not very much, I'm afraid. So it's the Professor! Is he thinking of having another shot at private space travel?"

"No! He's having it."

"Mary-Lou, what on earth do you mean?"

"He's gone—he and another man. Dad heard of it through a pal of his and cabled me so that I could come and tell you. They took off the day before yesterday about 4 a.m."

Joey set down her cup with an emphatic bang. "Do you mean that after the fiasco of that first effort those two are mad enough to have gone off again?" Mary-Lou nodded, her mouth too full of lemon biscuit for speech. "Then they should have been certified! They escaped death by nothing less than a miracle last time! Oh, *men*! From first to last, they're nothing but a trial—with a few exceptions to prove the rule, of course," she added, calming down a little.

"I'm sorry, Auntie Joey, but Dad says it's true. I brought the cable for you." She pulled it out of her pocket and handed it to Joey.

Joey scanned it quickly. "H'm! Not much here, of course. Where did you get the date and time from, by the way? It doesn't give them here."

"From *Die Berner Zeitung*. Marie Kauffman has it regularly. Her father writes for it. It was just a tiny paragraph at the foot of a column. I generally take a dekko at it and that just leaped to my eyes. That was when I decided I must see you pronto—and alone, if possible."

"I see. Now what do I do about it? Tell Ruey when they get back from Montreux? I don't want to spoil the poor child's holiday. No; you be quiet, Mary-Lou. I must think this out. Have a biscuit—clear the plate, so far as that goes. But keep quiet and let me think."

Mary-Lou's worst worry was over, now that Joey knew,

116

and her appetite had returned. She took that lady's injunction literally and sat back in her chair, munching Anna's superb biscuits and feeling happier every moment. Joey sat thinking hard and fast. At last she sighed, picked up her cup and drained it.

"That's better!" she said. "I needed that!"

"What have you decided?" Mary-Lou asked.

"To let it ride for the moment. This," she tapped the cablegram on her lap, "gives us the bare fact that those two maniacs have gone. We'll wait for a letter before I say anything to Ruey and the boys. But if only I had the Professor here, I'd scorch the very ears off his head!" she added vengefully.

Mary-Lou was almost herself again. She broke into a peal of laughter at Joey's final sentence and nearly upset the few remaining biscuits.

"Oh, I mean it!" her hostess said. "Mary-Lou, whatever you do, never marry a one-idea'd man!"

"That's easy enough to promise," Mary-Lou said disdainfully. "I don't mean to marry at all."

"Ye-es. That's what I used to say when I was your age. And now look at me!"

"Did you really?" Mary-Lou asked. "Then how on earth did you come to change it—and in such a wholesale way, too?"

"I suddenly woke up to the fact that I couldn't manage without Jack," Joey said simply. "It's no use making downright statements of that kind, my lamb, for you never know what the future may bring forth. And now, enough of that! Is your dad writing by airmail, d'you think?"

"Oh, sure to! I'm only surprised that he sent the cable to me. I should have thought he'd have cabled direct to you."

"No!" Joey was positive on this point. "He knew it was our half term, didn't he? He'd know that it was more than likely I'd have the girls here. He would never have risked it."

"No, he wouldn't, of course—though I hadn't thought

of it before," Mary-Lou agreed. "But a letter's different. I expect he'll write direct to you, so be on the look-out for it."

"Trust me for that! And thanks for letting me know so soon—and for telling me privately. Now I'll have time to think things over before even Len gets back. That's all to the good!" She paused before adding gravely, "Do you know, Mary-Lou, I'm just a little afraid of Len when I'm worried or upset about anything. Try as I may, I find it hard to keep things from her. She's so abnormally quick at sensing my feelings."

"She gets it from you, doesn't she? You always were able to get inside someone else's skin and know exactly how they were feeling. Len has it from you all right."

"You have it yourself, if it comes to that," Joey said. "I know how much you helped my three that last term you were at school. Oh, I've never asked any questions since the Head warned me off; but she did say that, thanks in the main to you, my girls were all on the right road."

Mary-Lou was scarlet. "I didn't do much beyond butting in good and hearty and telling each one of them exactly where she got off."

"Evidently it was what they needed. It's made a big difference to them."

"Oh!" Mary-Lou then changed the subject. "Any more coffee in that pot? Dad's cable came with the early morning letters and I was so worried, I couldn't eat. By the way, how's the time going? Bill gave me an hour. She knows, by the way. I had to explain why I had a cable at all."

"What did she say about it?" Joey asked curiously as she poured out the last of the coffee and hot milk and passed the cup to Mary-Lou.

"Very much what you said, omitting the advice about marriage. Tell me, Joey," she left out the title, which was only brevet rank, as Joey had given her leave to do when they were alone, "how do you think Ruey will take this?"

Joey pursed her lips. "Not as you would have taken it.

118

And certainly not as our own gang would if Jack had been mad enough to want to go space flighting. I know she feels that she and the boys don't really count with him. It isn't as bad as it might have been."

"I think it's bad enough," Mary-Lou said stormily. "If he was as mad on space as all that, at least he might have waited until his children were grown up and able to fend for themselves!"

"I know," Joey responded. "But this really is an obsession with him. People who are otherwise sane enough *can* become obsessed by some idea and then they are apt to forget everything else. Carried to its logical end, I suppose you get complete dissociation and one form of insanity."

"It's awfully hard luck on his belongings, though," Mary-Lou replied. She glanced at her watch, gave a cry of horror and jumped up. "Mercy! Where has the time gone? I must fly. I'll be along this afternoon and if you don't want Len to find out that you're worried, you'd better think up something to occupy us fully. I don't mind telling you that coming to you has made me feel pounds better, though I'm still not happy about Ruey and the boys. He is their father, after all. Auf Wiedersehen! Be seeing you! I simply must fly!"

Mary-Lou fled and Joey went to the study to become, apparently, immersed in her new book. She had wheeled the trolley out to the hall and pushed it into the kitchen when they left the salon for Mary-Lou to collect her belongings, so there was nothing left to tell that she had had a visitor. When Len looked into the study, having taken Bruno round to the back entrance, she found her mother frowning over a page of typing with such absorption that she scarcely received a reply to her announcement that Bruno had been going it.

Len drew her own conclusions, and quietly slipped out, much to Joey's relief. She was still afraid in case that acute young woman should guess that there was something wrong. She remained absent during the whole of lunch, when Felix and Felicity came down from the playroom to join them. Len set down this abstraction to the new book, attended to the twins herself and never guessed what alarming news had come to Freudesheim during her absence.

Chapter 14

JACK IS BORED

DR Maynard approved of his wife's decision to keep the latest news of Professor Richardson's hare-brained doings from Ruey for the present, so the half term weekend was a thoroughly enjoyable time for everyone, the two elder Maynards excepted. Between the Professor's antics and his anxiety about Naomi Elton, who still remained hanging between life and death, Jack himself could enjoy nothing. Joey managed to put most of her worries at the back of her mind during the daytime, though Len regarded her thoughtfully more than once. None of the others even guessed that there was anything wrong. Margot, in particular, had thrown off her melancholy and was gayest of the gay. Len had found an opportunity on the Sunday to pass on the Head's hint, and once her sister had grasped the point, she hailed it with an enthusiasm that promised trouble for any members of Vb who did *not* come into line.

"I'll get hold of Francie and Pen and Tina and—and—let's see—oh, Primrose, of course! Ruey's always on hand—well, she is an adopted sister in one sense, isn't she? Now who else can I think of?"

"I've noticed that Maria Zinkel seems to be always pretty well up on marks," Len suggested.

"You're right; Maria really does work. Well, that's," Margot counted on her fingers, "seven of us to—to leaven the lot. I wonder if we can do it?"

"Of course you can, now you're keen enough. That lot are mostly sheep. They'll run baa-ing after you if you only set them off."

121

"What a picture!" Margot giggled. "I only hope you're right. Anyhow, I'll do my best and saints can't do more. But of course there are always the folk who don't care, like Prudence Dawbarn, for instance."

"Oh, bother take Prudence! She *is* an ass! Priscilla is going ahead all the time now. Doesn't Prudence care that her twin looks like being VIb while she is only Vb if Auntie Hilda carries out her threat? And she will, you know!"

"I know she will. She doesn't say things like that and not mean them! Well, I'll do my best, but if you ask me, Prudence is nothing but a silly kid who won't grow up."

There the talk ended; but Margot returned after the half term holiday full of the latest plans for making Vb go to work in real earnest. To her surprise, when she began to sound some of the others, she found that she was by no means the only one to feel that way. Quite a number of the others had been so appalled by the Head's lecture that they had decided to pull up.

Margot contrived to get the girls she had mentioned together and retail Len's remarks to them. Everyone agreed with what she said and even Prudence Dawbarn had been sufficiently impressed to behave herself during the Wednesday night preparation, though no one put much faith in her ability to continue.

Meanwhile, the letter containing the news about the Professor, with such details as could be found out, had duly arrived at Freudesheim and Joey read it with growing dismay. Finally, she thrust it across the breakfast table to Jack.

"Jack! Read that!" she commanded.

He laid down his own correspondence. "What's all this in aid of? You seem agitated."

"So will you be. It's from Roland Carey. You read what he says and give me your considered opinion. I'll pour you some more coffee while you're at it."

He passed his cup and then concentrated on the letter. As he read, he frowned more and more blackly. When he

122

reached the end, he turned back and read it through again. Then he folded it and whistled softly.

"Here's your coffee," Joey said. "Well?"

"Anything but well! This is a nice mess! I never thought he would really go off again after what happened last time. That lunatic had the narrowest shave of drowning last time. I see that after the first twelve hours no signals have been picked up so far as they know and no one has seen their track, either. Good heavens, Joey! That may mean anything!"

"Including their complete extinction—I know. Didn't the Professor care in the least for his own children?"

Jack finished his coffee, pushed the cup aside and began to put on a pipe. "In one way he did. He did realise that they were dependent on him. So far as money goes, he made every arrangement he could—including appointing you and me as their guardians."

"I'm glad he had that much sense!" Joey said stormily. "But that's the least of it. Didn't he know that this business would probably make orphans of them? And, so far as he knew, it left them utterly alone in the world, poor kids."

"If you ask me, when their mother died, they *were* more or less orphans. Well, I suppose we must decide what we are to do about letting them know of this."

"I suppose they must know? But we can't keep it from them. I think you'd better try to get on to Laurie Rosomon and ask him to go and see the boys. I'm not worrying so much about them. Roger's seventeen and has plenty of sense. Roddy's just a kid and won't grasp it all. It's Ruey I'm worrying about. She's very sensitive under that couldn't-care-less manner of hers. Should I ask Hilda to let her come over here to me this evening?"

Jack picked up the letter again and glanced over it. "I think I'd wait a day or two longer. Roland says that he'll send on any news he gets as soon as possible. Nothing's definite yet. If nothing more comes through by Sunday, I'll get on to Laurie and you can send over for Ruey and

123

the other girls to come and spend the day. Hilda will let them come, once she knows what's involved."

"I'm only too thankful to wait," Joey answered. "I know Ruey doesn't feel as she ought for her father, but even so, it'll be a shock to her, poor kid!"

So it was decided, and for the rest of the week Ruey was left in blissful ignorance of what might be in store. She was working furiously, determined to back up Margot with everything in her. Margot was working equally hard, and so were the others. Margot's suggestion that they should all pitch in and give everyone concerned a shock over the next fortnight's form-list had appealed to a good many folk. Games were off for the thaw was continuing. This being the case, those young ladies who were games-mad decided that they might as well attend to school work and so, with any luck, miss the awful disgrace of being turned into a kind of annexe to Inter V next term. The staff could scarcely believe their senses when girl after girl showed up exercises properly done, or answered on lessons decently prepared. As Miss Wilmot remarked, they crossed their fingers and hoped it might go on.

Meanwhile, out of school hours Len was having a hard time of it with Jack. Having had to do without her mentor for the best part of five days, the Junior Middle had amassed a fine body of questions to ask her. As Len had laid it down firmly that anything not to do with rules must keep until they were in the dormitory, Jack never got answers to more than three at once. Since she had an appallingly inquiring mind, she had generally added quite that number to the residue by bedtime and, as she told Wanda crossly, she never seemed to be able to get level.

Wanda giggled. "But I am glad it is Len you ask, for I could never tell you all that you want to know," she remarked.

"Well, that's what I said at the beginning," Jack pointed out—it was Wednesday and therefore English day.

The Junior Middles and the Juniors had an hour's preparation each evening. Then someone took the Juniors to their own common room and stayed to oversee their activities while the Junior Middles, who were made up of Upper IIIb and Lower IIIa, went to theirs next door and amused themselves as they chose, so long as they made no noise. On this particular evening, most of them were busy at the tables, rearranging stamp, postcard and crest albums, making scrapbooks, drawing and painting, or playing games.

Jack's own hobby was machinery. When her father stripped the car down, she was generally to be found helping and up to the elbows in grease and dirt. As no one was prepared to allow her to mess about with either of the school cars and Karen would never have permitted any of them to fiddle with her own special machines in the kitchens, Jack was unable to indulge herself.

On this evening, Wanda and Co. were busy with their collections. Margaret Twiss and her special crowd were enjoying a fierce tiddlywinks tournament. Most of the others were busy with one game or another, and though Rosemary Wentworth had called Jack to share their snakes and ladders, Jack had declined.

"I call it a soft game. It takes you ages to get anywhere and then just as you look like getting Home, you land on the head of that long snake and have to go slithering right to the bottom and start all over again!" she said. "Not for me, ta!"

"Oh, well, suit yourself. I think it's a gorgeous game," Rosemary said, half offended. "Come on, people! Bags me the blue!"

They settled to their game and Jack was left to her own devices.

Upper IIIb were playing a slightly rowdy Impertinent Questions, but as there were twelve of them at it already and no ordinary pack of cards contains more than fifty-two, there was no room for even one more. Those left were engaged in their own ploys. Jack stood near the door staring round. She was bored. Presently, she slipped quietly out of the room and went wandering about until she finally reached Hall. It was in darkness when she opened the door, but the electric light switches were just inside. Jack slid in through the smallest crack, after the fashion of little girls, switched on the lights and looked round. Suddenly, her face lit up too. She had never found time yet to examine the honours boards round the room properly. Now was her chance! She shut the door behind her and started off. She knew well enough that she had no business there at that time. If she were caught it would mean a lecture and also a bad conduct mark. Never mind! At least she had found something to do!

She went slowly down the first wall, pausing before each board and reading the names and achievements of girls whom she had never known. Most of whom, indeed, she had never heard. She was not to know till later that Josephine Mary Bettany was her beloved Len's mother or that Frieda Marie-Louise Mensch was the mother of Gretchen von Ahlen in her own form. She did pause before Marie von Eschenau. Surely she must be some relation of Wanda's!

"I'll ask Van when I see her again," Jack thought.

It had taken her a good three weeks to get accustomed to the fact that Wanda sounded her W like a V, and she still saw the name as written with a V.

She was so absorbed in what she was doing that she never heard light steps coming down the corridor. The first thing she knew was that the staff door at the top of Hall was opened and a voice exclaimed, "A Junior here —and at this hour! Come here, child! What are you doing here?"

Gwen Parry, the games prefect, having finished most of her work for that evening, had suddenly remembered that Miss Burnett had given her a list and asked her to put it up on the notice board in Hall some time before Prayers that evening.

Jack had suddenly come on a group of names she knew, headed by that of her own Aunt Gay. There it was, in letters of gold for all to see. "Gabrielle Elizabeth Lambert.

First holder of the Margot Venables Prize". But why had no one ever told her? And what was the Margot Venables Prize, anyhow? Jack had been much too thrilled to heed Gwen's footsteps and she was well caught. She jumped violently at the sound of the games prefect's voice and turned red.

"Come here at once!" Gwen said, stuffing the precious list into her blazer pocket.

Jack trailed up Hall until she was standing before the big girl—Gwen stood five foot nine and was built on a generous scale—one foot rubbing up and down the back of the other leg, a trick of hers when she was embarrassed.

"What are you doing here?" Gwen demanded.

"I—I—don't know," Jack faltered.

"Jack Lambert, isn't it? Well, Jack, why aren't you with your own crowd?"

"I don't know," was all Jack could find to say again.

"Where are the others?"

"In our common room."

"Then why aren't you with them?"

Once more it came. "I don't know."

Gwen was a pleasant girl, but she had a quick temper. Moreover, she was beginning to remember Jack in detail. Wasn't she the youngster who had played that silly trick in the staff bathroom? No doubt the monkey was planning something equally mad for Hall. What she could find to do was beyond Gwen, but she had no intention of leaving such an imp to her own devices. Besides, "I don't know" was no sort of answer. Jack must know well enough what she was doing there.

"Come out!" she said severely. "Follow me!"

Jack followed her, Gwen having snapped off all the lights and shut the door with great firmness. The second form room was close at hand and empty. Gwen marched an unwilling Jack into it, switched on one light and then went to seat herself before the mistress's table. She motioned Jack to stand opposite her and set to work to find out the explanation of this conduct.

"Which is your form?"

"Lower IIIa," Jack replied.

"Has no one told you that you kids aren't supposed to be in Hall by yourselves unless anyone in authority sends you there?"

Jack nodded.

"I—I wasn't sliding!" Jack ventured.

"I should hope not!" Gwen's voice was chilly in the extreme. "What were you doing?"

Silly Jack decided not to mention the honours boards. It seemed such a mad thing to do, to go there by herself just to read the names of a lot of people most of whom she had never heard of. She kept silence and Gwen was to be excused for thinking that she had been up to no good.

"Well," the prefect said, having thought it over, "you may take a bad conduct mark for breaking a rule. Another time, please remember that you little girls are expected and trusted to remain in your own common room till the bell rings for the end of prep. Now, as you seem to have nothing to do, you had better come up to the prefects' room with me and I'll find you something for the last twenty minutes or so. Come along; and in future, please remember what I've said."

She got up, walked Jack upstairs and established her in a chair at the far end of the table with the injunction to read a story book and see if she could keep out of mischief for the rest of the time.

The other prefects in the room raised their eyebrows at Gwen as high as they would go, but the games prefect merely shook her head and said, "Later!" in an undertone before burying herself in the poems of André Chénier.

Jack sat, silent and miserable. It was the longest twenty minutes in her experience and she was thankful when the bell rang and Gwen sent her off to wash her face and hands, ready for Abendessen.

Jack went. But when she was well away from the prefects' room, she stopped short and stamped her foot. "I hate and loathe and despise Gwen Parry!" she said aloud. "But I'll get even with her! I wasn't doing any harm and I think she was a beast to treat me like this!"

Then, as she heard doors opening and the noise of many feet scuttering along to get an early place at the toilet basins in the Splasheries, she gave up breathing fiery threats and scuttled downstairs intent on the same object.

Chapter 15

A Bad Reputation

JACK continued to boil internally whenever she remembered Gwen's remarks to her. And then to drag her to the prefects' room and keep her there for ages with only a stupid book to look at! And to crown everything by that bad conduct mark!

"It's beyond the beyonds!" Jack said to herself, quoting an expression of her mother's, when she was in bed that night.

To make matters worse, Len had, for once, not been on hand. A lecture on mountaineering was to be given at St. Mildred's by a well-known climber and the three top forms had been invited to share it. So Jack was alone with no one to advise her or help her to see things straight.

Nor could she have Len next morning. That young lady was on the Thursday early practice list and had to hurry off as soon as she was ready to put in as much time as she could.

The next Sunday crowned all, for Len and the other three went home in the morning. There had been no further news of the Professor and the Maynards felt that it could be kept from his family no longer. He had given none of them much reason to love him, but all the same it came as a shock, and Joey was glad that she had asked for her own girls as well as Ruey, for they proved to be the girl's best comforters. As she rather pathetically told Joey when they had to go back to school that night, even though they weren't really related, she did feel that they were sort of sisters.

"I'm glad," Joey said. "And remember, Ruey, that

there's nothing really definite yet. He may turn up again. You never know. Chin up, old lady! Things are never so bad but they might be worse!"

It was the right line to take with a girl like Ruey. Petting she would have hated, especially if it made her cry. As it was, she went off feeling consoled and strengthened. By the time it was as sure as it ever could be that her father had really gone, she was able to face it sanely and pluckily.

All this was unknown to Jack Lambert, who took it as a personal affront that she was deprived of Len's services for yet another day. And Len, full of sympathy for Ruey and working to the top of her bent during school hours, had little attention even for Jack.

Margot sought her sister out some days later to ask what on earth they could do with Prudence Dawbarn and her followers! So far as anyone could judge, they had given up their first efforts and were sliding back to their old ways of not caring what happened so long as they could scrape a bare 45 per cent on the fortnight's average and so save themselves from the worst trouble.

Len thought it over. "I think you'd better let Priscilla know," she said finally.

"Well, I can try, I suppose," Margot returned. "My own opinion is that Pru Dawbarn wants a red-hot grid-iron shoved under her! That might make her sit up and take notice!"

"I'll say it might!" Ruey exclaimed, she and Con having come up in time to hear Margot's final remark. "She really is a pest, though. If it weren't for her, I'm positive the rest of that crew would work a little harder, anyhow. As it is, they pull down our form average every time and it isn't good enough!"

"Put Priscilla on to her," Len repeated. "It might do the trick."

"Will you do it—or Con?" Margot asked. "It might come better from you. You two are in the same form as Pris."

"Better make it all four of us," Con said. "It'll carry more weight that way."

It was left at that. The four of them caught Priscilla during the next walk and put it to her earnestly that something really must be done about Prudence.

"I'll talk to her all right!" Priscilla said vengefully when she had heard what they had to say. "What an ass she is! Dad said if she didn't get a better report this term, he'd take her away and send her to day school. I know Pru thinks she can get away with anything where he's concerned, but she won't get away with that one."

"Well, do your best with her," Margot implored. She's an awful ass and she won't listen to us though we've done our best. You have a shot!"

Priscilla promised. In passing, it may be mentioned that whatever she did say to her twin certainly had some effect.

Meantime, the days were going by and Jack, try as she would, had still not found out how to "get even" with Gwen Parry. Gwen herself had forgotten all about the affair. In any case, the thaw had ended abruptly when a bitter wind brought back frost and snow, and when it blew itself out the school returned joyfully to winter sports, so the games prefect had little reason to bother with Jack, who continued to sulk in a way quite unlike her usual self.

The frost continued to the end of the third week after half term. Then the Föhn began to blow and the thaw came in earnest. Everywhere was soaking with heavy mists, showers of rain, and snow gone badly to slush. There was no going out for three days, but the fourth dawned bright and sunny, with blue skies and a fresh breeze from the west. And that was the day that Jack got her idea at last. A sillier notion could hardly have been found, but it was all she could think of.

At Frühstück, the Head announced that since the roads and paths were drying up at last, and the weather forecast was good, all lessons would be excused that afternoon, and, instead, the school would go for walks. Jack decided that it must be now or never! Luckily for her, lessons for the Junior part of the school ended at twelve-fifteen. If she could only evade the rest she might manage it.

They got through the morning well, but even those stately young ladies, the prefects, were excited as they streamed through the corridor to their Splashery. Once there, they talked hard, discussing which route they should choose. Gwen, using French with an abandon that would have made Mlle gasp with horror, put her hand into her locker to yank out her heavy, nailed boots without bothering to look at them. They came with a jerk and their owner was well doused by an impromptu shower-bath.

Gwen yelled with surprise and dismay, and the rest dropped what they were doing to surround her and proffer help and suggestions—this time, in English, except for the half-dozen or so who came from other countries and employed their own native languages.

"What on earth—!" Josette exclaimed. "How under the sun did that happen?"

"Gwen—Gwen! Hier ist ein Handtuch!" Marie Zetterling cried, coming with her own towel.

"Your stockings are simply soaked. You can't possibly go out like that," Josette said. "Here, Catriona! Fly up to Gwen's dormy and fetch her a clean pair. Drenched doesn't begin to describe these!"

Between them, they managed to set her to rights, but when it came to the boots, it was a very different matter. Jessica had emptied them into one of the toilet basins and announced that there was at least half-a-pint of water in each. They were soaking and quite impossible to wear.

"Well, that's stymied my walk all right!" Gwen said disgustedly.

"No; you take the same size as I do, don't you?" Monica Caird asked. "Here's my old pair that I forgot to take home at the end of last term. Put them on and we'll get Karen to dry yours out in the furnace room. We do want to settle this for ourselves, don't we?" she added, appealing to the rest.

They certainly did—Gwen most of all. As she said, she had no wish for whoever was responsible to know how well her nasty trick had come off!

"But just let me get my talons into her and I'll see that she remembers it to the end of her days!" she said viciously, as she pulled on Monica's old boots while Josette, picking up the maltreated pair, ran to the kitchens with them to coax Karen the cook to set them in the furnace room to dry out.

Finally, they were able to set off for their walk not more than ten minutes later than the others. As Prefects, they might go unescorted and they made full use of their freedom to discuss the practical joke.

"It's some Junior or Junior Middle trying to be funny!" was the decision they came to unanimously.

"Yes; but why hit on me?" Gwen demanded plaintively. "Who hates me badly enough to do such a nasty thing to me?"

No one could say. Gwen was a popular person as a rule. If she had a quick temper, it soon blew over and if she had been in the wrong, she was always ready to say so and apologise. The prefects could find no explanation. One or two were of the opinion that it should be reported, but Gwen stamped hard on that idea at once.

"Certainly not! It's only some little ass trying to be clever, though I can't see why I should be the victim. But for goodness' sake let's deal with it ourselves if we possibly can and not drag the Head or Matey into it!"

"But can we?" Monica Caird asked seriously.

"Well, Mary-Lou and Co. dealt with Ailie and her crew when they crammed Lost Property with oddments from everyone, whether they were left lying about or not. That affected everyone. This affects only me. Oh, no, Monica! We'll settle the thing ourselves, please."

They all agreed in the end. Nothing was to be said to the staff, but the prefects as a body were prepared to deal to the limit with whoever it was who had played such an unpleasant trick on Gwen.

At the same time that the grandees of the school were coming to this decision, Margot was confiding in Len that at long last Prudence Dawbarn seemed to have made up her mind to behave herself.

"Not before time, either!" she added. "I'm most awfully gratefully to you for thinking of putting Pris on to her. Thanks a lot, Len!"

"Rot! You'd have tried to help out if it had been me!" Len retorted. "I'm thankful something has pulled it off. Now let's give it a rest."

With this worry off her mind, Len had a little more time to look round. On thinking matters over, she realised with surprise that since the half term she had really seen very little of Jack Lambert. She might have settled down, but surely she couldn't have got through all her questions so quickly?

"Not like her," Len thought. "I'd better make a point of giving her a few minutes to herself when we're changing for the evening. Jack is the kind of kid that will always bear watching!"

With this in mind, she hurried over her dressing and when she was ready, made the rounds of the cubicles to inquire if anyone wanted any help. She began at the far end. Finally, she reached Jack's abode. And the instant she parted the curtains, she knew that something was wrong. Jack jumped so violently that she knocked her comb down. When she had picked it up, she showed the Senior a very red face and refused to meet her eyes.

This was so unlike Jack that Len instantly knew that she had been up to no good. She said nothing however, but she merely asked, "Like me to give you a hand with your counterpane?"

She spoke in French, the language for the day, and Jack mumbled, "Er—oui, merci!" which was about as much as she could manage at that point. Why had Len come to her like this, all of a sudden? Jack, with a very bad conscience, couldn't understand it and rather wished she hadn't. However, even if she had been rude enough to say it, she

135

hadn't the French for it. She took her end of the pretty counterpane; Len took the other; together they folded it neatly and hung it over the back of the chair.

"Now she'll go!" Jack thought. But Len didn't.

Instead she leaned up against the bureau and asked gently, "And what is the trouble, Jack?"

Jack's eyes flew up to Len's face despite herself. "I—I—" she stammered.

The gong sounded and Len, leaving it for the moment, marshalled the others into line and sent them off downstairs. Then she went back to Jack. In that one moment when the black eyes had met hers, she had glimpsed a certain naughty triumph mixed with apprehension and she meant to get to the bottom of it.

Jack was standing where she had left her and if ever a girl looked guilty, that girl was she.

"This is partly my fault!" Len thought. "I knew the imp needed looking after and I've been so busy with Margot's affairs, that I've left her to carry on by herself and heaven only knows what she's been doing!" Aloud she said, "Well, Jack, do you know the answers to all your questions?"

As this was not what she had expected, Jack was surprised into saying fervently, "Oh, no!"

"Then why haven't you come to me?" Len queried. "I know I've been away for a few days lately, but that didn't mean I wasn't ready to tell you what you wanted to know—if I could, that is—when I came back. And now, what have you been up to?"

Jack fidgeted with her fingers. "The—the gong has rung for Kaffee und Kuchen," she reminded Len at last. And her French was weird and wonderful.

For once, Len took no notice of it. "I know it has," she said. "All the same, neither of us is stirring fom here until I know just what you've been doing."

Jack stole a glance at Len from the corner of her eyes. She looked very determined. The Junior gave it up. "I—I filled Gwen Parry's boots with water," she blurted out in English.

Len's jaw dropped. She, too, resorted to English. "You did what?"

"Filled Gwen Parry's boots with water," Jack repeated, rather wishing herself at the other side of the world.

"But—but why?"

"'Cos she was horrid to me. She called me 'child' and said, 'you kids' and 'you little girls', just as if we were all beetles and not nice to know!"

"Well, considering what you've done, I should say she wouldn't think you very nice to know," Len said severely. "When did this happen?"

"When I was in Hall, looking at the honours boards."

For once, the self-possessed Miss Maynard was completely flummoxed. She made a wild dive after her vanishing self-possession and got hold of it firmly. "When were you looking at the honours boards?"

"It was the Wednesday after half term in the evening after prep. I'd nothing to do and all the rest were busy and I was bored, so I went to Hall to have a good look at the boards 'cos I'd never really had a chance before and I always wanted to." Then, suddenly forgetting that this was not just a pleasant chat, she added eagerly, "Oh, and Len, d'you know what? I found my Aunt Gay up on one of them!"

That nearly finished Len. She had an instant vision of Gay Lambert as she had known her, pinned up on one of the boards. However, she knew what Jack meant right enough and, in any case, that young woman was calmly confessing to a flagrant breach of rules. Len attended to Jack's morals at once.

"Didn't you know that no one is allowed in Hall out of hours except for a special reason?" she demanded.

Jack's excitement vanished. She nodded.

"Then why were you there if you knew you were breaking rules?"

"I wanted to read the boards properly."

"But, bless me, there are plenty of times when you can do that without breaking rules!" Len exclaimed. "As for playing such a disgusting trick on Gwen because she did what any prefect would have done, I simply don't understand it. I never thought you were spiteful, Jack!"

"I—it wasn't meant as—as spite," Jack faltered.

"Well, that's what it looks like. It was a horrible trick to play on anyone, whatever she had done."

"I s'pose Gwen will be mad at me again. But I was mad at her and she was mad at me first. She gave me a conduct mark, too!" Jack said aggrievedly.

"How do you feel about it now?" Len asked gravely.

Jack thought. "I—well, I never thought about it's being a nasty thing to do. I—I'm sorry I did it now." Then, in rather faltering tones, "I—I s'pose I'd better go and tell her I—I'm sorry. She'll be in the Speisesaal, won't she?"

Len sat on this at once. Gwen would hate a public scene, however much Jack might enjoy it—and Len made no mistake. Inwardly, Jack was revelling in the idea. It would cause a sensation! She could just see Margaret Twiss's eyes popping out of her head!

"You can't go and make a scene in the middle of Kaffee und Kuchen. You'd better go to your common room and I'll fetch Gwen to you. Come along and let's get it over."

Jack followed her meekly to the Junior Middle common room where Len left her while she went to call Gwen. Josette's eyebrows went sky-high at the sight of her young cousin coming in so late. Len apologised to her and then said, "I really want to speak to Gwen if I may."

"What's biting you?" Gwen asked amiably as she got up from the table and followed Len into the corridor.

"It's about your boots," Len said.

"My boots? Don't try to tell me that it was *you* who filled them chockful of water, for I shan't believe you."

"Of course it wasn't me!" Len cried indignantly. "I hope I've more sense! It was that little lunatic, Jack Lambert. She has just confessed to me and she's waiting in their common room to confess to you. Let her down as lightly as you can, Gwen. She's simply a silly little ass who seems to do the first thing that comes into her head."

138

"But what have I done to move her to such hatred?" Gwen demanded.

"Apparently you caught her in Hall out of hours and talked 'as if she were a beetle and not nice to know'," Len quoted with a sudden chuckle. "What's more, you put the lid on everything else by giving her a conduct mark."

Gwen looked stunned. Then she began to laugh. "I remember! I thought it wasn't safe to leave such an imp to her own devices, so I marched her back to our room and kept her there till the end of prep. But surely she doesn't bear malice for an everyday thing like that?"

"I don't think she does—normally. So far as I can gather, she had nothing to do and she was bored. I must see what I can suggest in the way of a collection or hobby that she will like! She's not a bit girly—more like a boy."

"She looks it, with that cropped black head of hers! OK, Len. I'll deal with her. You go and get your Kaffee und Kuchen and leave her to me."

Len went thankfully and Gwen marched off to find Jack, whom she speedily reduced to a proper sense of her wickedness. However, after awarding her another conduct mark, besides telling her that when the boots were dry she could clean them properly, she added, "Len tells me you aren't interested in the usual kind of collections. What does interest you?"

Jack, who had been smarting under the lash of Gwen's tongue, gave her a startled look before she replied, "Well —machinery—cars and engines and things like that."

Gwen nodded. "I see. Well, my eldest brother used to be crazy over railways when he was your age and we have a lot of his stuff put away in the boxroom. If you would like to have it to start you off collecting on your own, I'll bring what I can manage next term— some rails and an engine and some trucks and carriages. What about it?"

Jack flushed and her eyes shone. "I say!" was all she managed to get out.

Gwen nodded. "Very well. And though we've been talking English all this time, I'd better remind you that

this is a French day. Now come along and get what Kaffee
und Kuchen you can before everything has to be cleared
away. And another time, do think before you play a
practical joke on anyone!"

Jack went to the Speisesaal with beaming face. It had all
looked very unpleasant; but thanks, she was sure, to Len,
it had turned out not so badly after all. And Gwen really
was rather smashing, all things considered.

What Jack did not see just then was that she was rapidly
gaining for herself a bad reputation for mischief and
something far more unpleasant was to come of all this —
and that before so very long.

Chapter 16

THE JOKE THAT WENT WRONG

"WHERE are you off to, Jack?"

"Only to Matron to get my chilblains done," Jack replied from the doorway of Lower IIIa, and Barbara Hewlett nodded.

"OK. But for goodness' sake get back as fast as you can. You know what Bertie's like about being punctual and all that!"

"I'll scram!" And Jack scuttled off to seek Matron —something she should have done as soon as she had finished her cubicle work.

Matron was a pleasant creature and though she reminded Jack that she should have come earlier, she let it go at that and the small girl was able to be seated in her place, her work before her, before Miss Bertram arrived to take duty with them. This was Saturday morning, and from nine till ten they were supposed to do their mending, after which they might finish preparation left over from the previous night, write home letters or, if they preferred, read their library books. Lower IIIa very rarely did the last. It generally took them all their time to cope with mending and prep.

Jack, with her right hand thickly padded and bandaged to prevent her scratching and breaking the chilblains which afflicted her fingers, was excused from mending. Several envious looks came her way.

"But oh, how fortunate you are, Jack!" Renata sighed. "I have a big hole in the heel of my stocking to mend and also three buttons to sew on to my blouse."

With her fingers stinging and tingling from Matron's lotion, Jack made a face.

141

"I don't call chilblains lucky!" she retorted. "You just try them! You itch horribly and you want to scratch and you just can't by the time Matron's tied you up. Well, look at me!"

Before anyone could obey her, there came a warning hiss from Wanda von Eschenau who was standing behind the door, "doing doggy", as they called it.

"Stop talking! I can hear her coming!" With which she shot back to her seat.

All chatter ceased, and when Miss Bertram entered they were all in their own places, looking as if butter wouldn't melt in their mouths. They stood up, chanting in unison, "Good morning, Miss Bertram!"

"Good morning, girls!" Miss Bertram returned as she went to her table to take register. She sat down and flipped open the book "Sit down, and be quick about it!" she said sharply.

They sat down, one or two of them glancing quickly at each other. Usually, Miss Bertram was the jolliest person alive. Today, her lips were set in a thin line and her brows were drawn together in a heavy frown. If they had been old enough, they might have seen that her pretty pink colouring had gone; but people of eleven and twelve rarely do see such things. All they saw was that "Bertie" was not her usual cheery self and they had better behave like baby angels as far as they were able.

She took register, and when she had finished she handed it to Arda Peik to return to the office, bidding her see that she came straight back without any dilly-dallying on the way.

Arda went off, looking faintly scared. The rest, having been told to get on with their work and not waste time, proceeded to do so. Only Jack, with the stinging of Matron's lotion almost gone and the easing of the itching and burning of her chilblains for the present, at any rate, turned to her French verbs feeling fairly content.

Miss Bertram, glancing round her flock to make sure that they were all well employed, dropped on her at once. "Jack Lambert! Where is your mending?"

142

Jack stood up. "Please, Miss Bertram, Matron says I mustn't even try until my chilblains are properly healed." She held up her hand as proof.

"Do you mean to say those chilblains aren't healed yet?" Miss Bertram snapped.

"No," Jack said ruefully.

"Then you must have been scratching them again! It's high time you had a little self control!"

"But I haven't—I couldn't!" Jack returned quickly. She did not mean to be pert, but the swiftness of her reply sounded like it.

Miss Bertram flushed a dull red. "That will do! No impertinence, if you please! Very well. Go on with your preparation and don't waste any more time."

Jack sat down again, looking both bewildered and indignant. Miss Bertram, with all the warning symptoms of a coming bilious attack full on her, leaned an aching head on one hand and set to work to correct the Second form's English grammar. Arda came back and received a sharp reprimand for taking so long and went to her seat with an expression that matched Jack's.

It was some time before Lower IIIa forgot that Saturday morning. Margaret, dropping her scissors with a crash that sent a knife through the aching head, was rebuked with a severity that turned her scarlet. Hanni Unsel having brought white wool when she needed pink to darn a tiny hole in a vest looked at the said hole with resignation and put the garment away. And Miss Bertram, with a nasty taste in her mouth, black spots before her eyes, the feeling of having rocks in her tummy and a splitting headache to crown it all, gave up her corrections and went round to inspect their work.

The Chalet School prided itself on turning out every girl a good needlewoman. Mlle taught it and her own sewing was as exquisite as you would expect from a Frenchwoman. No matter how much any girl might loathe it, sew she must and sew well into the bargain. The staff all did their best to keep the girls well up to the mark. All the same, Lower IIIa felt this morning that Miss Bertram was needlessly fussy. She made Margaret Twiss and Rosemary Wentworth unpick their laborious darning and begin all over again. She commented most unlikely on Renata's attempts at stitching up a torn buttonhole and nearly reduced Gretchen von Ahlen to tears by her scathing remarks on that small person's effort at mending a glove finger. By the time the bell rang for Break, very few people had contrived to attend to their preparation. As for home letters, Jack was the only one to try to begin and, thanks to her padding and bandages, her writing was so awful that she was badly scarified and felt ready to fight with a feather by the time Miss Bertram had finished with her.

In short, Lower IIIa drew long breaths of relief when at last they were dismissed to seek their milk and biscuit. As for Miss Bertram herself, she piled up her exercises and left the room wondering if she could manage to reach the haven of her own bedroom without collapsing in public.

Luckily for her, she walked straight into the arms of Matey, who took one look at her face and marched her off to bed with orders to stay there until the attack was over. Miss Bertram fought hard against the medicine Matron gave her, pleading that she would be sick if she tried to swallow anything.

"Very well; be sick! You'll be all the better for it!" was all the comfort Matey had for her. All the same, she was never left until the worst was over and, feeling very empty, but distinctly more comfortable, she was tucked up with a hot-water bottle and quickly turned drowsy.

Naturally, Lower IIIa knew nothing about this and they relieved their minds freely once they were well away from anyone in authority.

"Bertie's been simply ghastly to us the whole day!" Barbara summed it up as they got ready for their walk. "I only hope she's not taking us now!"

"It's Ferry and two prees—Clare and Jessica," Renata informed her, having taken the trouble to look at the list.

144

"Oh well, that ought to be better!"

"I'd just like to get back at Bertie for being so horrid to us!" Margaret declared. "I haven't finished even one of those stockings yet and it's not fair."

"You aren't the only one," Rosemary said gloomily. "And I haven't even looked at my rep. I left it specially for this morning, but I hadn't a minute for it."

"I said you were lucky, Jack," Renata observed to that character with deep reproach in her voice. "You have got all your prep done."

"Yes; but did you hear what she said about my writing?" Jack demanded. "It isn't my fault I can't write decently just now. It's those beastly—"

"Who's that using forbidden slang?" The Head Girl appeared among them. "You Jack Lambert? Pay your fine into the box and remember that you may not use 'beastly' to describe anything but an animal. Off you go!"

Well caught out, Jack went off looking like a thunder cloud to drop her fine into the box, feeling that all the world was against her.

There was no doubt about it; that bilious attack of Miss Bertram's had a good deal to answer for. Lower IIIa were badly upset and even a good brisk walk in the fresh breeze and the sunshine did little to soothe them. No one told them of their form mistress's illness, or they would have excused her at once. Matey reported it to Miss Annersley.

"All the same," she wound up, "she has these attacks once or twice every term and she tells me that they come in the holidays as well. I think she ought to see Dr Morrison. He might be able to give her something to clear them up."

"I'll talk to her tomorrow," the Head agreed. "It may be some quite little thing that the right medicine or a minor operation would set right. Leave it to me, Gwynneth, and I'll do what I can."

So there it was left. One or two of the brighter spirits did notice that their form mistress was absent from the school over the weekend, but they took it for granted that she had gone to stay somewhere.

Monday morning came and Miss Bertram, still rather pale, but otherwise looking as usual, appeared to take register. Matron had been urgent that she should take the day off, but Miss Bertram declared that she felt fairly fit now and anyway, with Miss Andrews in San with influenza, she couldn't be spared. So she arrived among her lambs, who were feeling far from friendly towards her. They were sadly conscious of the fact that repetition, French verbs and dictation words were very sketchily prepared, except in Jack Lambert's case, and all expected trouble of one kind or another before the day was over. Jack and a few of the others were coming round, but quite a number felt positively hostile and when Miss Bertram greeted them with her usual smile and a bright, "Guten Morgen!" they replied primly and stiffly, "Guten Morgen, Fräulein!"

"Setzt Euch, meine Kinder!" the mistress said, setting them the example. She opened the register and then tugged at the drawer in her table to get her pencil for marking. The drawer seemed to stick. She gave it a hard jerk, it came open and—out leapt a long green snake, landing full on her chest. Though no one knew it except one or two of her colleagues, Miss Bertram had a horror of snakes. She was still not fully recovered from Saturday's attack and the suddenness of the thing was too much for her. She gave a queer, choking sound and collapsed in a heap on the floor while the toy snake fell to the far side of her chair.

The form was stunned into silence for exactly one moment. Then pandemonium broke out. Only four people of the twenty-five made any attempt to keep their heads. The rest either yelled or burst into tears. Wanda, leaping from her seat, grabbed a big bowl of narcissi and emptied the contents—flowers and water alike—over the mistress. Barbara Hewlett with a cry of, "Give her air!" snatched up the first thing that came handy and fanned Miss Bertram vigorously. Rosemary Wentworth dashed at the windows and threw them all wide open while Jack

146

rushed to the door, intent on finding someone who could deal with this alarming event.

It was a blessing for everyone, Miss Bertram included, that Len Maynard, sent on a message to the office, was passing their door just as Jack wrenched it open. Len promptly forgot the message and hurried in to see what was wrong.

"What's wrong here?" she demanded sharply. Then she saw Miss Bertram lying in a heap, her skirt soaking and bestrewn with Wanda's flowers and her face white and waxy.

"Stop that noise instantly, all of you!" she exclaimed. "Stop crying, you little ninnies! That won't do any good! Now—"

She knelt down by the unconscious mistress, and began to turn her on her back. "Oh, is she dead—is she dead?" Margaret sobbed.

"Nonsense! She's only fainted!" Len said firmly. "Jack, go and fetch Matey and be quick about it! Lend me a couple of blazers to put over her, some of you. Pile up those books, Barbara, and lift her feet on to them. Who on earth's been strewing flowers over her? I must say you strike me as a bit previous! What's that thing by the chair? Pick it up, one of you, or someone will be tripping on it. Now Wanda, come and help to rub her hands—like this."

Thankful for someone who knew what to do, Lower IIIa calmed down a little. Len and Wanda chafed the icy hands after Len had spread the dozen or so blazers proffered over Miss Bertram, and mercifully Jack found Matey quickly. She blurted out what had happened in two sentences.

"Please, Matron, will you come at once. Miss Bertram's ill, I think."

"How?" Matron demanded, hunting in her cupboard.

"I think she's fainted."

"Right! Who's in charge?"

"Len Maynard."

"Very well. Come along!" Matron had found what she

147

wanted. She only paused to snatch a blanket from her bed and load it on to Jack. She went by the front stairs and Jack followed, her arms full of blanket, while Matron unscrewed the top of the smelling salts she had found and was all ready as soon as she was in the form room.

Matey wasted no time. She knelt down by Miss Bertram, who was beginning to show a few signs of life, and held the smelling salts under her nose. Miss Bertram gave a deep sigh, stirred, opened her eyes and looked round vaguely.

"What's wrong?" she asked faintly.

"You fainted," Matron replied in matter-of-fact tones. "Len, go and find Gaudenz and ask him to come here, will you? Then go to the office and ask Miss Dene to ring up for one of the doctors. I don't know what made Miss Bertram faint—"

"I think it was this," Barbara interrupted with great lack of manners. She held up the toy snake which someone had put on the table. Miss Bertram opened her eyes, saw it, gave a suppressed yelp and looked like fainting again. Rosemary grabbed the thing quickly and tossed it across the room while Matron, with her usual presence of mind, said, "Some stupid child tried to scare you with a toy snake and, considering how very poorly you've been all this weekend, I'm not surprised you fainted. I thought you shouldn't have come into school today. Yes; I know the staff are shorthanded, but you weren't fit for it. Now," as the steady clump-clump-clump of big boots announced the arrival of the man-of-all-work with Len, "Gaudenz will carry you up to your room and we'll see what a few hours of bed will do for you. Ah, Gaudenz!" as that worthy stumped in. "Miss Bertram has not been very well—just a little faint. Will you help her up to her room, please? I'll come with you and see to her. Len, you take charge here until someone else comes." She stood up and glared round the room. "And I may as well inform you here and now, girls, that as soon as I have settled Miss Bertram, I am going straight to Miss Annersley to report all this to her."

She turned and stalked out of the room after Gaudenz, who had scooped up Miss Bertram in his brawny arms and was carrying her off as if she weighed no more than one of her pupils. Len closed the door after them and took charge promptly.

"I don't know what you people ought to be doing," she said, "but the bell will ring for Prayers in a moment, so line up against the door and don't forget your hymn books. Quickly, please!"

Lower IIIa obeyed her instantly; but as they took their places, quite a number of people cast meaning looks at Jack Lambert, though they said nothing. "Now march quietly to Hall, and after Prayers, come back here and wait quietly till someone comes to you," Len said. "After what Matron said, I rather think you may be prepared for it to be the Head. There goes the bell! Forward—march!"

CHAPTER 17

MISS ANDREWS IS KEPT QUIET

HAVING been forewarned by Len, Lower IIIa transformed themselves into the nearest thing to young cherubim they could contrive. Miss Annersley noted as she came along the corridor that there was no sound at all coming from their room. She could well believe that the morning's events had given them all a nasty shock. Well, whoever was responsible for this joke must learn that such things were not acceptable in the Chalet School. For once, she was thoroughly angry and the culprit was in for an unpleasant time. She reached the door, turned the handle and swept in, her MA gown billowing portentously round her.

Lower IIIa came to their feet in one movement. The Head stalked up to the table and took her place behind it. "Sit down!" she said briefly.

They sat. Every eye was fixed on her face and, as they marked the glint in her eyes and the grim set of her mouth, most of them shivered inwardly.

"Who was responsible for putting that snake into Miss Bertram's drawer?" she asked.

There was silence. No one owned to it and Miss Annersley's expression became severer than ever.

"I see I must go round and ask each of you separately," she said. "Barbara Hewlett, did you do it?"

Barbara jerked to her feet. "No, Miss Annersely. I never saw it before," she said earnestly.

"Thank you; that is all I want. You may sit down. Angela Sartori?"

Angela, blushing to the roots of her fair, fluffy hair,

denied any knowledge of the thing with vehemence. She was told to sit down and the Head passed on to Mollie Rossiter. One by one, she asked them separately and everyone said more or less the same thing. She came to Jack and, looking down into the black eyes which had lost their usual twinkle for once, asked the same question.

"Jack Lambert, is this yours and did you play this silly trick?"

"No," Jack said sturdily. "I don't know anything about it. It isn't mine."

A distinct hiss came from the back row. Jack went red and Miss Annersley removed her gaze from the cheeky little face which was unnaturally grave just then and looked along the row.

"Who made that noise?" she asked sharply.

Redder even than Jack, Renata van Buren got to her feet. "Please, I did," she said, speaking her native Dutch in agitation. "It was—"

She got no further. Miss Annersley held up her hand and the words trailed off. "Come out here, if you please, Renata."

Renata stumbled out of her seat and up the room to the foot of the low dais on which the table stood. The Head eyed her up and down in silence until she was ready to scream. Finally, she spoke.

"I see you understand the habits of snakes."

It was all she said but, spoken in those tones, it was more than enough. The Head looked at her for another thirty seconds or so. Then she turned back to the girls, with an effect of ignoring the very existence of the sinner who stood before the dais and wished the ground would open up and swallow her at once. The rest all glued their eyes to their desks, except Jack, who was still standing and looking at the Head almost defiantly.

"You may sit down," the Head said. "Wanda! Do you know anything about it?"

Wanda bounced up, her eyes sparkling and every curl on her head crisping with rage. "No, Miss Annersley and neither does Jack! She isn't a liar!" she exclaimed before anyone could stop her.

For an instant, the Head's expression softened at this championship. Jack flashed a grateful smile at her friend. Then the moment was over and the Head was saying, "Very well. Sit down, please, Wanda. Arda Peik?"

Arda replied with a simple, "No!" and the Head went on.

When the last girl had replied and no one had owned up, she leaned back in her chair and surveyed them all. "So we have a coward and a liar in this form!" she said; and every girl in Lower IIIa squirmed literally as well as mentally.

No more was said for a full minute, but more than one girl darted a look at the seat where Jack was sitting with her head held high. None of them were angels, but during the term Jack had earned for herself a well-deserved reputation for doing the maddest things. Miss Annersley knew as clearly as if they had spoken what they were thinking. They had made up their minds that she was to blame for this latest affair. Considering Jack's exploits, she could hardly blame them.

She spoke again. "I am very disappointed, girls, and deeply grieved as well. I will give you until this evening after preparation. If, during that time, the girl who did this will come and own up she will, of course, be punished for her naughtiness in playing such a trick on a mistress; but I will forgive the lie. If not, then until whoever it was does come to me, this form will be in silence out of school hours. That is all. I think your first lesson is dictation. Open your books, please. Renata, you may go to your seat. I will speak to you later in the study. Barbara, which passage had you to prepare?"

Renata crawled back to her seat, keeping her eyes on the floor. Barbara brought the book used for dictation in Lower IIIa and pointed out the passage. Then it began. The less said about it, the better. Not even Jack, who had prepared it thoroughly, did much with it. Nor did they do any better over French verbs which followed.

It was the same with the rest of their lessons that

morning. They were not allowed to go for their milk and biscuits as usual. Mlle told Barbara to go and ask Karen to send their elevenses to them by one of the maids, and she herself remained with them until a prefect arrived. Not until the end of morning lessons were they alone for one minute, for the mistress who had just taken a lesson waited for her successor to come and this rubbed in the seriousness of the whole affair as very little else could have done. But at last twelve o'clock came and they were told to put their books away and go and get ready for their mid-morning walk.

Upper IIIb, who usually went with them, were detained by a little matter of history with Miss Charlesworth, so Lower IIIa had the Splashery to themselves. They began to change their shoes and pull on their coats and berets. Then Renata, who was by way of being a leader among them, came up to Jack who was dragging her beret over her smooth black head.

"I have very little to say," she began abruptly. "Most of us know that you play mad tricks and until you own up to this one—and we are sure that it can only have been you, for none of us would think of such a thing—we are not going to have anything to do with you. We do not like liars and cowards here."

"You may count me out on that!" Wanda cried, putting an arm round Jack, who looked stunned at this attack. "I don't believe Jack had anything to do with it. And if it comes to tricks, indeed, you are no angel yourself, Renata! You are as likely to have done it as Jack. But she didn't hiss like a snake when you said you did not!" she added; and had the satisfaction of seeing Renata go scarlet.

"I don't say Renata did it," Barbara added her own quota, "but I will say this. We have never known Jack to tell a lie. She's always owned up instantly. Until it's proved that she did it, I'm going to believe her."

Jack swallowed hard, for this was unexpected. "Thanks a lot!" she muttered.

But if Wanda and Barbara were prepared to believe her, it was more than the rest were—with one exception.

The exception was the last one Jack would have expected. Margaret Twiss, called on to agree with the verdict of the others, mumbled, "Well, she's never told a lie before and if she says she didn't do it, I don't s'pose she did."

All the same, it was a hard day and Jack found out that it is easier to gain a bad reputation than to lose one. After afternoon school, Barbara and Wanda had to go for music lessons, so she was left alone; for Margaret, after making her surprising statement, did nothing more.

They were in their common room and she was beset by a number of the others, all begging her to go now and own up to the Head that she had done it.

"If you don't, we'll all be in silence from tomorrow morning," Rosemary wailed, "and it isn't fair to make all of us suffer just because you're a funk!"

"I'm not!" Jack retorted furiously. "I'm no more a funk than you are!"

"Then why don't you go and tell the Head?" Renata demanded.

"I didn't do it, I tell you! And I've told no lies, either. If I went to the Head and said I had, that would be a lie and I'm not going to do it! You shut up, Renata! Whoever else did it, it wasn't me! So now!"

"She's hardened; that's what it is," Mollie Rossiter said severely. "Well, stick to it if you like, Jack Lambert, but don't expect us to have anything to do with you until you go and own up!"

The Head waited in her study in vain. No one went to her and, in consequence, their doom came on them next day. For the rest of the week they were to be in silence. This meant that they might not talk to anyone apart from lessons. Nor might anyone talk to them. In their free periods, instead of amusing themselves as they chose, there was always someone with them. They took their walks in silence. In the evenings, someone came and read to them while they did either needlework or handcrafts. It was a dreadful week!

It was a bad week for the staff, too, for they had two mistresses on the sick list. Miss Andrews had a very sharp attack of influenza and for two days ran a temperature that caused both Nurse and Matey to look very grave. When at last it broke, she was so weak that they kept her very quiet and she knew nothing about the latest in school politics. Dr Morrison, summoned by Matey to Miss Bertram, sent her off to the Sanatorium for an X-ray, the result of which was that a minor operation was declared to be the only means of putting a stop to her periodical bilious attacks. It was performed on the Wednesday and she came through well; but it meant that the school must do without her for the rest of the term.

"Still," Joey remarked when she was visiting the patient on the Saturday after, "if this means no more bilious attacks for you, it's been well worth it! You stop fussing, Joan, and be thankful for a little peace and rest!"

In the meantime, the tale had begun to leak out to the remainder of the school, as it was bound to do. Anne Lambert went to the Head as soon as she heard it and begged to be allowed to talk to Jack. The Head was very sorry for her, but, as she pointed out, she could make no exceptions for anyone. Len Maynard, going with the same request, fared no better.

Anne had been easily squelched, but Len was a different matter.

"I know those little ninnies in Lower IIIa are certain it was Jack," she pleaded, "but I'm positive that if she said it wasn't, then it wasn't. Jack doesn't tell lies. Oh, she's naughty, all right, but it's a nice naughtiness, Auntie Hilda."

"If naughtiness can ever be said to be nice!" Miss Annersley retorted. "Oh, I know what you mean. I've had it said to me before. The point is, Len, that I'm afraid that the result of the shock on Miss Bertram has made whoever it was doubly afraid to own up. It's silly, of course. In the long run, it's been all to the good, though I'm not letting them know that! At the same time, having dealt out a certain punishment to them, I can't break it for anyone. That would be most unfair."

"But Jack looks so awfully miserable," Len urged.

"If it teaches her, guilty or not, that you can't make a reputation of endless mischief for yourself and hope that it will be forgotten almost at once, it won't hurt her. She has to learn that sooner or later and the sooner the better. I'm sorry, Len, but Jack must put up with it. I can do nothing about it until Sunday. We'll see then," was the most the Head would say and Len had to go away, thoroughly dissatisfied.

On the Friday morning, Joey Maynard strolled into the study with a proposal that she should take Miss Andrews home with her for the weekend and see if that would help her to convalesce more quickly. She had come in her own little runabout and, if the mistress were well wrapped up, she ought to take no harm. The Head declined to agree until she had discussed it with Nurse and Matey. However, they both agreed with Joey. Miss Andrews was not making headway. Perhaps the change would help her. Anyhow, it was worth trying and one or other of them would pop in each day to see how she was, while Jack Maynard was on the spot.

"When he's there," Joey agreed cautiously.

In the end, Miss Andrews was bundled up in rugs and blankets and borne off in triumph for the weekend, with babies to amuse her and Joey's own brand of comfort and gentle amusements to combat the aftermath of depression always left by influenza.

It worked, as most of Joey's undertakings did. Sharlie Andrews left protesting that she wished they wouldn't bother her but just leave her to die quietly at school. By teatime she was feeling a little brighter and able to take an interest in a cup of tea and some of Anna's matchless fancy bread. She was sent to bed along with the babies; enjoyed the delicate supper Joey brought her and, later, fell asleep to the sound of that lady's golden voice as Joey, with the doors open, sat at the piano and sang song after song.

When Joey arrived next morning with a cup of early morning tea, she found a Sharlie Andrews who had a faint pink in her cheeks and looked bright-eyed. More, she announced that she was looking forward to breakfast and when it came, cleared the tray. By midday, she had managed to dress herself and, with the help of Joey's arm, staggered down the stairs and was ensconced on the big settee in the salon with small Cecil and the new twins to amuse her. An afternoon nap also helped, and by Sunday, no one heard anything more about being allowed to die quietly!

Mindful of Ruey's loss, Joey had previously begged for her four to come home to tea that day and they arrived shortly before sixteen hours, delighted to see the junior mistress looking like herself again, and full of chatter.

It was after tea while they were sitting together in the salon that it happened. Joey had been murmuring sweet nothings about bedtime for Cecil and the twins. Finally, she got to her feet and picked up little Geoff from the big playpen.

"Fetch Phil, Margot," she said, "and you bring Cecil along, Ruey. It's high time these babies were safely in their beds! You two can help me tonight. Len and Con, you see to Miss Andrews. I shan't be long and then we'll have a singsong when we three come back. Come along, girls!"

They left the room and Len, casting about in her mind for something to amuse the young mistress, pitched on the tale of the awful doings of Lower IIIa.

"You've missed something," she remarked as Con threw more logs on the fire.

"What?" Miss Andrews asked.

"The sad affair of Lower IIIa," Len said laughing. "It's really been very sad and it's not over yet, I'm afraid."

"What have they been doing?" Miss Andrews asked, laughing also.

"Don't you know?" Con demanded in some surprise. "I thought everyone did."

"No one's told me anything. Your father said I was to be kept quiet and my goodness, they've seen to it that I was! What have Lower IIIa been up to?"

Thus urged, Len launched forth into the tale. She didn't get very far. She had just reached the place where Miss Bertram had wrenched open her table drawer with such appalling results, when her auditor gave an exclamation.

"Oh, my goodness! I'd forgotten all about it till this minute!"

"Forgotten about what?" Con asked.

Len looked at her uneasily. "I was forgetting you'd been ill. Perhaps I oughtn't to go on. You're still supposed to keep pretty quiet, Mamma says."

"Keep quiet, indeed! It's all this keeping quiet that's done the damage! If only they'd told me sooner!"

Len and Con looked at each other in dismay, for Miss Andrews was not quiet now. Her cheeks were pink and she looked highly excited.

"I don't see what you could have done to help all this," Len ventured at last.

"But it wasn't them at all!" Miss Andrews cried, loudly and ungrammatically. "It was me—I did it!"

By this time, both the Maynards were convinced that Miss Andrews was ill again and running a temperature. She must be in a high fever to accuse herself of playing such a trick on one of her colleagues! They jumped up and tried to persuade her to lie down quietly on the settee until they could fetch their mother.

Little Miss Andrews, standing between the tall girls who towered a good six or seven inches over her, began to laugh. She could guess what they were thinking. But she sat down, much to their relief, and pulled them down on either side of her.

"No!" she cried. "I'm not delirious! And it is my fault, though if I hadn't gone down with flu when I did, I'd have remembered to remove the thing later on. That snake thing belongs to Anne de Guitry. She was playing with it during prep, the monkey. I confiscated it and serve her right! I put it in my blazer pocket, meaning to hand it over to Miss Dene later on. But by that time, I was feeling pretty bad. I went into Lower IIIa to leave their exercises for Monday morning. I was putting the sheets into the table drawer when the snake fell out of my pocket. I distinctly remember picking him up and ramming him in on top of the exercises. By that time, you see, I felt so awful, I wasn't very sure what I was doing. And then Matey met me and marched me off to San. No one's even mentioned it to me, thanks to this business, so of course I knew nothing about it. Oh, those poor imps!"

Len's eyes were shining. "I said all along it wasn't Jack Lambert! I knew she wouldn't tell lies, however sinful she might be in other directions! I didn't think any of that crowd would—not to persist in them, anyhow. I have a pack of them in my dormy, and I felt sure of them. And I didn't think the others were like that, either. Oh, thank goodness it's all cleared up at last!"

"You go on and tell me the rest of it," Sharlie Andrews commanded.

They told it between them. Joey and her helpers arrived towards the end and Len sketched a hasty outline for her, winding up by begging to be allowed to tell the Head when they returned to school.

Joey gave a chuckle. "We'll go one better! Margot, go and ring up Auntie Hilda and tell her I want her at once and she's to stay to supper with us. Off you go! Len, go and bring Miss Andrews a cup of coffee. She's all in and I don't know that Papa would quite approve of all this excitement for someone who was only begging to be allowed to die two days ago!"

"Die? Don't talk nonsense, Joey! I'm practically fit again. Oh, I feel wobbly still, and I won't insist on being allowed to go into school for a day or two yet. But I'm sure that by Wednesday I'll be all right again."

Miss Annersley arrived twenty minutes later and among

them they sorted out the entire story. Miss Andrews explained her share of it and apologised for all the trouble she had made.

"Though it wasn't altogether my fault," she wound up. "If you hadn't all been so keen on keeping me quiet, I'd have heard of it days ago and explained."

Miss Annersley laughed. "Oh, we'll all bear the blame for it! But oh, how glad I am to hear that it was all a mistake and *no* one has been telling lies! That really did worry me badly."

Margot looked at her with wicked blue eyes. "Well, if you kept Miss Andrews quiet, Auntie Hilda, you also kept Lower IIIa quiet and out of mischief for an entire week!"

Chapter 18

MARGARET OWNS UP

THE warned the four girls that they were to say nothing. She intended to see Lower IIIa early next morning and tell them herself and they could very well wait until then.

"In any case, they should all be fast asleep by this time," she said.

It was Len who was most affected by the fiat.

"I wish you'd let me drop just a hint in the morning," she said. "It would cheer them all up—especially Jack Lambert. That poor babe has had a doing this past week or I miss my guess!"

"I'm hoping it will be a lesson to her to stop and think before she plunges into any more hare-brained exploits," the Head said gravely. "At nearly twelve, she's quite old enough to know that there are certain things you don't do. In one way, I'm not sorry this has happened to her."

They were alone in the entrance hall, the other three having gone off to the Splashery. Miss Annersley smiled at the disconsolate face before her.

"I know you feel partly responsible for Jack. She certainly seems to imagine that she has a special right to you, for questions, anyhow. In that case, you must be prepared to harden your own heart when it's necessary. Jack has found out from this episode how hard it is to win back a good name if you have earned yourself a bad one. If she had not played all those pranks earlier in the term, no one would have thought her more likely to blame for the snake than anyone else. She's been paying for her own silliness."

"I see." But Len still looked dissatisfied and she went

161

up to bed very serious. However, her lambs were all sleeping peacefully when she looked in on them, so she gave it up and went to bed and to sleep herself.

Next morning, a message went round all the dormitories where members of Lower IIIa slept, bidding them come to the study at half-past seven. That was all, and every last one of them began to wonder frantically what new and awful penalties lay ahead of them. If only they had dared to talk, Jack would have been told what most of the occupants of Pansy thought of her in good plain terms; but they dared not.

At twenty-past-seven Len made the rounds of the cubicles. Then she sent everyone to line up by the door and marched them off downstairs to the study. They found quite a number of the others already in the little passageway, waiting. Even as Len got her flock into order, the remainder arrived. They looked at each other mutely. Then Barbara ventured to stretch a point and ask Len to knock for them. Len grinned at them, tapped, and then went off on her own occasions, leaving them to it. A voice called to them to come in and, headed by Barbara, who had been shoved into that place by the rest, they filed in solemnly. No one looked up. They were all far too apprehensive as to what this summons meant.

When the last girl had pressed in and the door was shut, Miss Annersley said, "Good morning, girls!" Every head jerked up and they looked at her hopefully. Her voice had lost its iciness. She was smiling at them and her eyes were very kind.

They returned the smile uncertainly as they responded, "Good morning, Miss Annersley!" They were still not quite sure. Next minute their uncertainty was gone, for the Head was laughing as she said, "I'm afraid I can't ask you to sit down, there are too many of you, so you must stand. I sent for you to tell you that the mystery of the snake has been cleared up at last. I know that none of you is to blame and I apologise most sincerely to you all for not believing you after you had assured me that you knew nothing about it. I am very sorry indeed that I doubted you—any of you!"

One or two people involuntarily glanced at Jack Lambert and Renata, at least, blushed furiously. Jack took no notice, she was gazing at the Head.

"Please," she said, "are we to know how it happened?"

"Not at present. It was someone quite different and if things had been as usual, it would never have happened."

Their jaws dropped and they stared at her round-eyed.

She laughed again. "Do close your mouths, girls! You look like a school of stranded codfish!"

Every mouth was shut with a snap, and most people went pink.

"I'm afraid," she went on, smiling at them again, "that the past week hasn't been very happy for any of you. However, it is over now. You are in silence no longer. And, best of all, I find I was utterly mistaken in thinking there was even one coward among you, and that—"

"Wah—hah—hah!" It burst out from their midst and they all jumped. Margaret Twiss was howling like a baby and fumbling madly for her handkerchief.

Miss Annersley was off her chair in a flash. "Margaret, my dear child! What is the matter? Why are you crying like this? I've told you that we know now that it was none of you who—"

"B—but it was me! It was!" Margaret wept loudly, her words so mixed up with her sobs that none of the girls could make head or tail of what she was saying and even the Head, with all her experience, could gather only a little here and there. "I—I s—saw Miss A—andrews p—put the snake into the d—drawer and I never said anything even when the rest b—blamed Jack for it! Wah —hah—hah!"

The Head acted promptly. "Run along now, girls. One thing, before you go! You are to say nothing at all about this until I have seen you again. You understand? Then run along quickly!"

They went, leaving the sobbing Margaret a safe

prisoner in the Head's arm. They were too stunned by all these happenings to say much. Even Jack, once they were safely in the common room, only remarked most maddeningly, "I said I hadn't done it! P'r'aps you'll believe me another time!"

When they had gone, the Head put her howling pupil into a chair and became busy with some papers. At the end of five minutes, she spoke very quietly, but very firmly.

"You have cried quite enough, Margaret. Dry your eyes and come here to me."

Margaret stumbled to her feet, screwing the damp ball which was her handkerchief into each eye and still heaving with sobs. Miss Annersley took the sodden affair from her and dropped it into the wastepaper basket. Then she got up and marched the weeper off to the tiny cloakroom which opened off the study. She turned on the taps, produced a clean towel, and briskly bade her wash her face.

Margaret obeyed and the Head, back at her desk, rang up the kitchen on the inter-house telephone and then sat back, wondering what weird confession she was to hear now! When Margaret finally appeared with a clean face, though eyes and nose were still reddened and swollen, she merely nodded.

"That's better. Now come and sit down and tell me all about it." A tap sounded at the door and she rose, saying quietly. "Wait a moment!"

One of the maids handed her a small tray with a beaker of steaming milk on it. She took it with a word of thanks, closed the door again and came back.

"Now, Margaret, before you talk, drink this. You'll feel better then."

Margaret, still hiccoughing at intervals, choked the milk down and found that she did, indeed, feel better. The Head smiled at her.

"Now tell me all about it," she said kindly.

Margaret gulped once or twice. Then the whole sorry story came tumbling out.

"I—it was Wanda being so pally with Jack right from the

start. I always wanted her to be pally with me, but she never was. And then she and Jack were chums and I—I hated Jack and—and was nasty to her. And when everyone else thought it was her had hidden the snake I was glad, and I didn't say anything though I knew all along it was Miss Andrews, 'cos I saw her doing it. Only when you asked us if we'd done it, I knew I should tell you, only I was so pleased 'cos Jack was in such a row and everyone thought it was her. And then they said have nothing to do with her 'cos she'd told a lie about it only I—I couldn't say she had, so I said if she said she hadn't, I s'posed we'd have to believe her, but I didn't do anything more about it!" Here Margaret stopped short and gulped hard again.

The Head sat in silence, thinking. "When did all this happen?" she asked at last. "And how was it that you were in your form room after school hours?"

"It was after Abendessen on Thursday. I suddenly remembered I'd left my new fountain pen on top of my desk so I went to get it before someone saw it and put it in Lost Property. The door was open and the light was on and I was afraid I was too late but I thought I'd go and make sure and then I saw Miss Andrews putting papers into Miss Bertram's drawer and the snake fell out of her pocket and she just crammed it in on top of everything else and shut the drawer and I didn't like to go in or say anything. And we have art first on Fridays and then geography and Miss Yolland takes register for us and so Miss Bertram can't ever have opened her drawer all that day and she had a pen with her when she came on Saturday and then she went away and the drawer was left and I forgot all about it until—until it happened on Monday." Margaret stopped again, out of breath for the moment."

"I see," Miss Annersley said. "Go on, dear. Anything else to tell me?"

"Well, when I saw how everyone was blaming Jack for it," Margaret resumed, growing more and more shaky on every word, "I just thought well it served her right and p'r'aps Wanda wouldn't be friends with her any more and there'd be a chance for me and you only asked me if I'd done it and I hadn't and I said so and it wasn't a lie! Only I've been getting miserabler and miserabler all the week till I just couldn't bear it any more, 'cos I knew it was all my fault, only by that time, I didn't dare say anything 'cos I knew the rest would be so mad with me for not telling sooner. And I was being such a pig to Jack and—and—oh, I'm so tired!" And poor, mixed-up Margaret began to cry again.

The Head acted at once. "Yes; you're worn out," she said gently. "Poor little girl! If Jack has been unhappy all this week, I'm sure you've been far, far unhappier, for you knew how wrong you were, both by acting a lie and by being so unkind to Jack. I know you didn't tell me any lies, but you did act one," as Margaret made a protesting movement. "Well, it's all over now. I'm sure it will all come right, now you have owned up. Stop crying, dear. I'm going to take you to Matron and ask her to put you to bed and keep you there for a good rest. Tomorrow you can begin again and try to do better. Would you like me to tell the rest what you have told me? They'll be wondering, you know."

"Please!" Margaret sobbed.

"Very well; they shall know about it. Now, Margaret, you must stop crying. It won't help and will only give you a bad headache. Come along with me. The rest will all be going into Frühstück now—I heard the gong sound a minute ago—so we aren't likely to meet anyone. You shall have a good sleep and then you will feel more like yourself again. I'll come to you later and we'll talk things over, but it's bed for you at this moment. Come along, dear!"

Margaret mopped her eyes. "Aren't you going to punish me?" she choked.

"No, dear. You've punished yourself quite badly enough. You'll never do such a thing again, will you?"

"Oh, no! Indeed I won't!" Margaret promised fervently.

"Then I don't think you need any punishment from me. Come along!"

She took Margaret upstairs and, when she had explained the thing in a few words, left her to Matron Henschell. As a prefect in her own schooldays, Barbara Henschell had mothered all the Juniors and she took charge of the bitterly repenting sinner capably and kindly. Margaret was whisked off to a tiny bedroom next door to Matron's own room, and comfortably tucked up in bed with a hot-water bottle to cheer her up.

"You'll be better alone for the present," Matron said as she gave the sheet a final pat. "Now don't think any more about it just now. Try to go to sleep or I'm afraid you'll have a very bad headache with all the crying I can see you have been doing."

Margaret was really worn out with her unhappiness, crying, and the long confession she had made, and she dropped off very quickly. The Head ran up to peep at her between Frühstück and Prayers and found her sleeping quietly, though her lashes were still wet.

It was halfway through the afternoon before she found time to run up again. By that time Margaret was wide awake and feeling herself after the long, quiet sleep and a delicious meal Matron had brought her. The Head asked how she was, felt head and hands and then, satisfied that the day in bed would see her as fit as ever on the morrow, talked to her.

Miss Annersley was very thorough. By the time she had finished, Margaret knew just how unpleasant her ways of thought and behaviour had been. But she was fully forgiven and promised faithfully to do her best never to be so silly and wrong again. The Head duly informed Lower IIIa what she had done. She also forbade them to mention the affair to Margaret by either word or look, once the girl had returned to them.

"I know she has sinned badly against our codes, and you are all feeling resentful at having an undeserved punishment, but how many of you would have done better

167

in similar circumstances? In any case, it is not for you to judge her. She had been and still is very unhappy about it. I trust you girls to do nothing to add to that unhappiness. Can I trust you?"

"Yes, Miss Annersley!" they replied in subdued tones. The Head left it at that, hoping they had all learned a lesson which they would remember for the future.

Chapter 19

Len Gives a Lead

Lower IIIa were in a nasty quandary. It was easy enough to promise to say nothing of what had occurred to Margaret. When the Head told them how really penitent she was, to the point of crying herself nearly into an illness over it, they were quite ready to forgive her. What was much more difficult was what they were to say to Jack.

"We really were nasty," Rosemary Wentworth remarked when some eight or ten of them were gathered together in the garden during that day's Break. "I don't see how we're going to make it up with her."

"You were the worst, Renata," Arda put in; whereat Renata went darkly red and said nothing.

"And neither Jack nor Wanda nor Barbara takes the least notice of us," sighed Mollie Rossiter, who had formerly been very friendly with Barbara and missed the friendship badly.

"I think," Gretchen von Ahlen spoke up, "that we were all very stupid. Jack never told a lie when she waxed Margaret's chair, nor when she gave Miss Burnett a bubble bath, and we should have known that she would not lie about the snake."

"It is so easy to think of that now," Arda sighed. "We must do something, I know, but I cannot think what."

Nor could anyone else. They had to go back into school and leave the puzzle unsolved for the time being. But it really was a worry and the whole form, with the exception of Jack and her supporters, were in an unusually humbled mood all day.

It must be owned that neither Jack nor the other two

did anything to ease matters. Jack had suffered badly during that week when she knew that most of the rest were blaming her for their punishment and accusing her in their minds of lying. Anything like a lie was utterly beyond her. She would blurt out the truth about her worst sins and take the punishment meted out; but no one could ever persuade her to colour anything. Black was black and white was white to Jack and she recognised no shades of grey.

Being a very human little person, she simply couldn't avoid casting looks of triumph at the others. Wanda was equally triumphant; and Barbara, who was a blunt creature, spoke her mind straight when Mollie ventured to say something about it.

"You shouldn't go round calling people liars when you've no reason to do it. Wanda and I knew Jack was telling the truth. You can't expect us all to have nasty minds!" she told her former friend.

All that day, the three went about together in their free time, chatting cosily—so far as you can chat cosily, when all talk has to be in a tongue native to only one of you and the third member of the party flounders wildly most of the time—and keeping the others at arm's length.

To make matters worse, only Renata could be described as a leader, apart from those three, and Renata was too overcome at what she had done to be much use. So the form were not a great deal happier, even though they had back all their old privileges.

Len, who might have noticed something among her own lambs, had an important violin exam that week and spent all her spare time practising and regarding the immediate future with shudderings and dread. She was sure she would fail, so Jack and Co. carried on their campaign without interference.

Len's exam came off on the Wednesday, and though she was still nervous about her results, she felt able to tell her sisters and Ruey when they clamoured to be told how she had got on that she thought she might have passed—just!

170

"I'll bet you've sailed through with honours!" Margot told her.

"No such luck! Oh well, it's over now and I can't do any more about it! Anyhow, term's nearly at an end. The holidays are just round the corner and I mean to have a jolly good time in them and enjoy myself. This has been a strenuous term," Len said.

Margaret came back into school on Thursday morning. She had had plenty of time to think while she was shut away, and the first result of her thinking came to light when she saw Jack coming into the common room before Frühstück. She went straight up to her, flushed and nervous, but determined to make what amends she could.

"Jack," she said, while Jack stopped short and stared at her in surprise, "I've been a perfect pig to you ever since you came—especially in not telling what I saw Miss Andrews doing with the snake. Will you—can you please forgive me and—and let's be friends?"

No one ever made that sort of appeal to Jack Lambert in vain. Out shot her hand, gripping Margaret's firmly. "Don't talk rot! Of course I will! Are you all right again?"

"This is German day. If anyone catches you two, you'll be fined," Barbara said detachedly, speaking in very careful German herself.

"Oh, bother! I forgot!" was Jack's excuse. "Well, tell me what to say in German and I may remember some of it for keeps!"

Len, who was busy herself, had rather expected to have trouble with her flock after the previous week's silence, but, now that her mind was free of worry about her exam, she was able to note that apart from Jack, Barbara and Wanda, no one seemed to have much to say.

It did not take her long to learn that things were difficult in Lower IIIa. She was hurrying down the corridor between lessons when she saw Jack come out of the form room to empty her painting-water—Lower IIIa had been busy with history charts under Miss Charlesworth—and Renata, who had just been on the same errand and was coming back, had to pass Jack. Jack tilted her chin as the other girl came and literally strutted off to the Splashery with her jar. Renata cast an appealing look at her, but got no return.

There was nothing to be done about it then. Len went past without making any comment, but she was determined to find out about all this as soon as she could. "What is all this in aid of?" she wondered.

She had to wait till the next morning to tackle Jack who, she felt sure, was at the bottom of it. It is true that young woman had five questions to put to her while they were changing for the evening, but all the others were in their cubicles as well and Len wanted to get Jack alone.

She managed it next morning. "Jack," she said quietly, "I know you've had a bad time over that stupid affair of Miss Bertram and the snake. I've been sorry about that, but in the first place I want you to remember that a lot of it was your own fault."

Jack stared at her. "How?" she asked bluntly.

"Well, you seem to have gone all out to get yourself a name for playing wild tricks on people. You must see that you were the first anyone would pitch on for another silly trick."

Jack considered. "I s'pose that's so," she said at last. "I hadn't thought of it that way. But I didn't mind that so much as the way they all—or nearly all, anyhow—thought I was lying about it. I don't lie!"

"I know that. All the same—" Len stopped there, but it was clear she had not finished and Jack waited, glancing at her with eyes that were quite serious.

It was an effort for Len to say what she did next, but she felt that something must be done about the state of affairs among the younger girls. She knew that Jack, at least, would listen to her. She fought down her natural shyness.

"Did you say your prayers this morning?" she asked at last.

"Yes; of course I did!" Jack stared at her in amazement. "Why?"

172

"All of them—properly?"

Jack nodded. She simply couldn't think what Len meant.

"You—you didn't miss out any of 'Our Father', for instance?"

"Of course I didn't! Why should I?" Jack demanded, thoroughly perplexed.

Len decided that she had said enough. "Think it over for yourself," she said as she turned to the door. "Really think it over, Jack."

Grasping that this surprising interview was at an end, Jack left the dormitory, still puzzled, and Len went after her, hoping that she had said the right thing.

It took Jack the best part of the day to work out her dormitory prefect's meaning. She thought over that little conversation off and on whenever she had a moment to spare, and Barbara and Wanda found her distinctly absent-minded all day. It was not until preparation was half over that she suddenly realised what Len had been talking about, and if anyone had been looking, they would have seen her go scarlet without any apparent reason.

"It's the bit about forgiving us our trespasses as we forgive them that trespass against us," she thought. "*Oh!*"

She did very little more preparation that night, but she had understood at last. Being Jack, once she got it, she must act on it. There was no chance until the next afternoon when they were having their rest period. Then Jack deliberately plumped her chair down beside Renata's, rather to the surprise of Barbara, Wanda and Margaret who followed her example perforce. Renata was even more surprised. That little coterie had been keeping well away from the others all the week.

Jack sat down, opened her book and read solidly for about five minutes. Then she turned to Renata, whose mouth fell open with the shock, and said, "This is a—a humdinger of a book! You'd better try to grab it after me."

"Jack! In French!" Barbara muttered with an agonised look at Josette Russell, who was quite near enough to have heard. But Josette seemed to be too deeply engrossed in her own book to pay any attention. She had had a brief chat with her young cousin just before Mittagessen, which may have accounted for it.

No more was said then; but later on, when they were walking in clumps along the highroad for their afternoon walk, Renata, accompanied by three or four of the others, came up to Jack's group.

"Jack," she said, paying no more heed to language rules than Jack frequently did, "we weren't fair to you about—about—you know what. You have never told a lie since you came to school and we should have believed you when you said you didn't put that snake thing in Bertie's drawer. We've been pigs to you. Will you please forget and let's all be pals again?"

Barbara gave up in despair. Anyhow, how could you expect girls to remember the sort of French needed for this unless it happened to be their own language?

Jack, looking her sturdiest, nodded violently. "Anyhow, it was partly my own fault 'cos I did such a lot of mad things earlier on. Len says so!"

"But we ought to have believed you, anyhow," Arda put in. "We were stupid not to. Only do let's stop all this and be like we were. This has been a horrid term!"

And that ended it. No one ever mentioned it again.

Later on, though, Jack contrived to grab Len. "I've—I've done what you wanted," she said. "I—I saw it when I'd thought about it. But, you know, I never would have done if you hadn't said it. I shan't forget again, though. Thanks a million!" Then, overcome with embarrassment, she scuttled off, leaving Len to get her breath. Jack's methods were startling.

Miss Annersley, who had been watching Lower IIIa with some anxiety, was relieved to see the entire body coming away from the netball courts next morning, all chattering like magpies.

"They're all right again," she said with a sigh of relief to Rosalie Dene who was with her. "I'm very thankful. I was worrying about them. However, something seems to have settled matters there. Mercy! What a din! Go and shut them up, Rosalie! We shall be having complaints about the noise they make if this goes on!"

Rosalie fled; but she gave her friend a meaning grin as she did so.

"Do you know what set Lower IIIa to rights?" Miss Annersley asked her that evening in the staff sitting room when, work for the day ended, the whole staff, except Miss Bertram, had assembled for coffee and conversation.

Rosalie nodded. "Though it's quite unofficial," she warned, while the others stopped their chatter to listen. "It was Len Maynard."

"Len Maynard? How did she do it?" the Head exclaimed.

"I gather that she had a talk with Jack, during the course of which she pointed out Jack's own sins to her and also made her see why she was making things worse by not forgiving the rest for their—mistake, shall we call it? I overheard Wanda and Barbara discussing it. They likewise remarked that they'd better stick to Len when they were in difficulties as she was such a smasher! Yes; I know it was forbidden slang, but as I was eavesdropping, though quite involuntarily, I felt there wasn't much I could do about it. I decided to turn a deaf ear and hope that Len herself would drop heavily on them if she caught them using such language next term. You know," she went on more seriously, "I know we were talking about our coming prefects, and we did decide that Va ought to supply us with a very good set when their turn came. I'm more convinced than ever about them, for Len is certainly helping to lead Juniors like Lower IIIa to come up as they should. And I'm not nearly so doubtful of Vb now, either. They have buckled to at their work, and even Prudence and Co. have done better this term."

"Prudence is never likely to be a prefect unless there's a startling change in her character," observed Miss Charlesworth. "But we look like having some difficulty in making a choice in Va when their turn comes. But, of course, the pick of that entire form is Len Maynard. She really is a leader, not only with her own form, where you might expect it, but evidently with the younger ones."

Miss Annersley smiled. "I agree with you. And," she added, as she got up to make her way to bed, "as long as we have leaders not only among the prefects, but in the lower Senior forms—such leaders as Len is proving herself to be—I don't think there can ever be much wrong with the Chalet School."